"**Y**OU'RE too honest to say you don't want me to kiss you," Karim said. "You have wanted to as much as I have."

"That still doesn't make it right," Fleur said. "Please let me go."

"No, Fleur, I can't." One of his arms released its hold of her and his hand moved up the slender column of her neck until his long fingers rested on her face, his skin brown against the whiteness.

With a mounting sense of danger, Fleur knew why she had always been so much on her guard with this startlingly handsome man. She loved him. Blindly, willfully and against all logic she loved this demanding, domineering stranger. And he was a stranger. Strange in his looks, his traditions, his culture, and in the way he intended to live his future. The thought of that future was the most frightening of all and she knew that unless she fought against her love for him, she would be irredeemably lost. . . .

Flower
of the
Desert

ROBERTA LEIGH

FAWCETT GOLD MEDAL • NEW YORK

FLOWER OF THE DESERT

© 1978 Roberta Leigh

Published by Fawcett Gold Medal Books, a unit of CBS Publications, the Consumer Publishing Division of CBS Inc.

A selection of the Doubleday Romance Library Book Club.

ISBN: 0-449-14150-0

Printed in the United States of America

10 9 8 7 6 5 4 3 2 1

One

FLEUR Peters took her place at the desk and waited for her class to file in. They would be giggling and several of them would be chewing sweetmeats, a habit beloved by many of her pupils, she had discovered, since coming to teach in Iran three months ago. She too had found herself nibbling between meals—something she had never done in England—for the nuts and raisins and the halva—a concoction of pounded nuts, almonds, and honey—were too delicious to resist.

Steps sounded outside, the door opened, and some twenty girls filed in. Used to the more boisterous behavior of British children, Fleur never failed to notice how docile these girls were by comparison, though when she had commented on it to Madame Nadar, the proprietor of the Nadar School for Girls, the woman had laughed.

"If you find my girls docile, wait until you meet those

who have not had the benefit of European teachers. After three months here you still do not appreciate that tradition dies hard—especially when it is also a part of one's religion."

"Until I came here I hadn't realized that women were kept subservient because of religious beliefs."

Madame had nodded. "The man is the leader in everything and women must defer to him—be he their father, their brother, or their husband. It is only as women have become more educated that they've started to question this."

"I should think so, too!"

"But there are still plenty of women who don't."

"Habit," Fleur snorted, her light green eyes flashing with derision.

"Habit and preference," Madame Nadar said. "It makes life easier for a woman if she knows she can always rely on a man."

"Yet *you* had a career as well as a husband," Fleur stated.

"I am considered an oddity by women of my own class," Madame had replied. "I was educated in France because my father was a diplomat and I married a diplomat, too. That allowed me to lead a more Western type of life. But when my husband died I was expected to return here and settle down with my women relatives in what you would, no doubt, call a harem. Instead I had the good fortune to start this school—but only because there were many wealthy families who wished to give their daughters some education without losing their own influence over them."

"They're making sure of that," Fleur had retorted.

"Two girls have dropped out of my class because their father objected to my giving them the short stories of Guy de Maupassant to read."

Madame had chuckled. "No matter. I have faith in your judgment, and if one or two parents object, it is their loss, not ours."

From then on the conversation had changed course, though Fleur thought about it when she returned to her classroom on the first floor of the large house which served Madame Nadar both as her school and her home.

It was only because the Persian woman had given her carte blanche on the way she taught her subject that she had left her job in a girls' school in Berkshire and come to Teheran. Rory's being here had had something to do with it too, though it would not have swayed her unless she had also found the right ambience in which to teach.

Occasionally there were times when homesickness made her regret her decision, but for the most part she enjoyed the climate, the unusual food, and the whole colorful way of life around her. There were also times when she was dismayed by the old-fashioned attitude of some of her pupils, for only one girl among the fifty whom she taught seemed to have an independent mind. As she also had literary talent and the ambition to develop it, Fleur went out of her way to encourage her.

Nizea Khan responded to it by making Fleur her idol, and her black eyes would glow with love when they rested on the tall, slender figure of her teacher, whose height and slimness was so different from her own rounded form.

Fleur knew of the girl's hero worship but saw it as no bad thing. Since she wished to encourage the girl to ask her parents for a university education, the stronger her influence the more likely she was to succeed.

Fleur was pondering this as her last class of the day filed in. Nizea was in the second row, her curly black hair held away from her face by a band of real gold. There was a matching gold bracelet on her arm, but otherwise she wore the standard dress required of her: a navy skirt and a white, short-sleeved blouse. Yet the voluptuous figures of the young Persian girls gave even these understated garments an unexpected sexiness.

"I finished the book you gave me, Miss Peters."

Nizea's soft voice caught Fleur's attention. Despite her gentle way of speaking, the girl had a determined streak, evidenced in the voracious way she read everything she was given, lapping it up like a hungry puppy so that she could beg for more.

"I doubt whether you can have absorbed it if you read it so quickly," Fleur reproached. "The first time I read *Pride and Prejudice* I took longer than a weekend."

"It couldn't have been a Persian weekend," Nizea said dulcetly. "Women have nothing to do except sit around and gossip and eat."

"You have a swimming pool, and you can also watch television shows," said the girl behind her, emphasizing this latter boon by naming several series which made Fleur shudder.

"I didn't realize American shows could be seen here," Fleur commented.

"They can't," Nizea said. "But Karim—my brother—bought me a videotape machine for my birthday and a hundred cassettes."

"Of American programs?" Fleur asked in dismay.

"Educational programs." Amusement lurked in the dark, liquid eyes. "But he gets the latest shows for his own machine, and I borrowed a few."

"Pinched them," said the girl behind Nizea again. "When your brother finds out he will lock his things away."

"Karim never locks anything away. We are not a household of thieves."

As the crime of thieving was—after the third conviction—punishable by having one's hand cut off, Fleur did not doubt this. It was a reminder that the newly acquired sophistication brought about by oil wealth was only a veneer and that a far more primitive civilization existed just below the surface.

"I think we've gossiped long enough," Fleur said firmly. "I suggest we turn our attention from Streisand to Shakespeare."

For the next hour she held her class enthralled, and only when the bell rang to terminate all lessons for the day did she motion Nizea to stay behind.

"I read the essay you wrote for me on Coleridge," she said, when the last of the girls had gone. "It was an excellent piece of work. There's no doubt in my mind that you'd pass your university entrance examination without trouble."

"There's no use passing it if I won't be allowed to go. My father believes a woman's place is at home with her husband and children."

It was on the tip of Fleur's tongue to say she had never heard of anything so outdated but common sense won the day. "Can't your mother make him change his mind? Or perhaps your brother? You give the impression that he is next in importance to your father in your household."

"So he is. But my father's word is law, and Karim would never oppose his wishes."

"Then it's up to *you* to persuade your father to change his mind."

"I can never do that," Nizea said sadly. "He has a will of iron." Great dark eyes studied Fleur intently. "He says that going to university would change me so much that I would no longer be his daughter."

"One can change without going to a university," Fleur replied. "You shouldn't concede defeat so easily. Remember that faint heart never won fair lady."

"Nor has a woman in our family ever won an education." Nizea still had her eyes fixed upon Fleur. "Perhaps if *you* spoke to my father it would help."

"I wouldn't be too sure of that," Fleur said drily. "Persian men aren't renowned for listening to their womenfolk."

"But you aren't his womenfolk! You are English and a stranger, and he would treat you differently."

He certainly would, Fleur thought silently. *He'd probably make sure I was deported!* But aloud she said: "I'll think about it and let you know."

"You are my only hope, Miss Peters. And you said yourself that if you believe in something you should fight for it."

"That doesn't mean I should interfere in family affairs."

"But what matters more than education? Am I not the most clever girl in your class?"

The girl struck a dramatic pose and Fleur smiled.

"You're certainly talented, Nizea, though if you go on like this I might think your acting ability is even better than your literary talent!"

The dark eyes flashed, but it was quickly over, and the girl was subdued again.

"I beg you to help me. All I want is a chance to use my mind. If you tell my father I am clever, he will believe you. He has a great respect for Englishwomen."

"How nice of him," Fleur said drily.

"Then you *will* see him?" Nizea asked, not appreciating the sarcasm.

"Yes, I will write to him today. But don't be too optimistic. If your father won't listen to you or your brother, I can't see his listening to me."

It was a statement with which Madame Nadar concurred.

"You are wasting your time, my dear. Mr. Khan will take no one's advice."

"Is he so sure he is always right?" Fleur asked.

"Even if he were wrong, he would never admit it. He is a man of the old school. There are not many left like him."

Fleur considered this a good thing but wisely refrained from saying so.

"Besides," Madame continued, "it will serve no purpose other than to make him more adamant."

"At least it will satisfy Nizea. Otherwise, she'd think I was letting her down."

"That is the only reason I do not ask you to desist from writing to him. But if he *does* see you, don't get carried away by your enthusiasm."

"It's my enthusiasm that makes me a good teacher."

"It could also make you a bad advocate when dealing with my countrymen. They like docile women."

Fleur smiled, at the same time wishing that Rory Baines were here to give her his opinion. Unfortunately, he had flown to London that morning and did not expect to be back for a week. Yet had he been on hand, he would probably have advised her not to get involved in any family contretemps. Rory was an international lawyer with a big oil company and was always careful never to make a misstep.

But having given Nizea a promise, she wrote to Mr. Khan that night, afraid that if she delayed doing so, discretion might yet win the day.

Unwilling to use Nizea as a go-between, she posted her letter, hoping this might persuade Mr. Khan she had asked to see him of her own volition. She did not expect a reply for several days and was astonished when an immediate reply was delivered by one of his servants, a dusky skinned man in livery. The letter was on thick, hand-blocked paper with gold initials. It had no address or telephone number, assuming that if you did not already have this information, you would never have had the temerity to write.

Pursing her lips, Fleur read the note which requested her to take tea with him on Sunday at four o'clock. There was no question as to whether this was suitable, and she knew that had she had another engagement, she would have been expected to cancel it. Mr. Khan was an autocrat of the old school.

"I still think you are wasting your time," Madame Nadar said when she learned of the quick reply. "But at least you will see inside a magnificent Persian home."

"How many wives does Mr. Khan have?"

"Only one. Polygamy is no longer allowed."

"But divorce is still very easy, isn't it?"

"Only for the men. Divorced women have no rights and are rarely allowed to keep their children."

"It's all so feudal," Fleur sighed and then changed the subject. "Should I wear anything special when I see him?"

"One of your pretty silk dresses, I think. And no hat. It would be a crime to cover that wonderful hair of yours. Mr. Khan can still appreciate a beautiful woman, and you will need every advantage you can muster if you wish to plead Nizea's cause."

Fleur bore this in mind on Sunday afternoon as she slipped on a pale chartreuse dress. It was of fine wool rather than silk, for despite the cloudless April sky, it was still cold. Even with a minimum of make-up, she still looked glowing with life, her red-gold hair a riot of waves around her head, her eyes a curiously pale green like those found in a Burmese temple cat. Had she possessed regular features, she would have been a chocolate box beauty, but her nose was slightly tip-tilted and her mouth generously wide with a full, softly curving lower lip. High cheek bones threw her eyes into prominence and apprehension at the interview ahead made them sparkle like green diamonds.

Afraid they looked too bright and intelligent, she lowered her lids to hide them. Her lashes were long and very thick and with narrowed eyes she looked as if she were trying to imitate a vamp. She opened them wide again and rubbed off both the small amount of eye shadow she had applied and also her lipstick. But nothing could mute her natural coloring and she abandoned the idea of trying. If Mr. Khan appreciated a woman's beauty, he would at least know enough to realize she had done little to improve hers and was very nearly the way God had made her.

"You're a walking contradiction," one of her girl friends had said to her a year ago. "You have the mind of a schoolmarm and the appearance of a showgirl. No wonder the poor men don't know where they are with you."

"They know where they're not!" Fleur had retorted. "And that's all that concerns me."

Wishing now for some of her friend's less obvious attributes, she went downstairs to the waiting taxi. She was a schoolteacher and she did not wish to be regarded in any other way—least of all by the autocratic father of one of her pupils.

Two

AT *five minutes to four, the taxi drew up* outside large, ornamental iron gates, their design so delicate that they resembled black lace. They were set in what seemed to be a white marble wall that stretched for some twenty yards on either side along the entire block.

The driver looked at her, and she knew he was waiting for her to get out but, determined to arrive in style, she pointed to the gate and with a shrug he sounded his hooter. A few seconds later the gates swung back, and they drove into a disappointingly small courtyard and stopped before another pair of gates. She paid off the taxi, and only as the car drove off did a servant appear to escort her through these gates into what was evidently the true inner courtyard of the house.

Here she caught her breath, overcome by the beauty around her. Everything was of shining white marble cunningly intermingled with blue and gold tiles to give it additional life. A fountain sprayed glittering jets of diamond-bright water into a wide, shallow basin lined with lapis lazuli. Persian plane trees with silver stems rose eighty to ninety feet in the air, their height telling her they had been here as long as the building that enclosed them.

The servant was moving ahead of her, and hastily she followed him into a circular hall. Small archways led from it, and they went through one of them into another circular room. This was more colorful and ornate, with Persian rugs gleaming like opals on the floor and several pieces of magnificent ivory-inlaid furniture ranged along the walls. She was glad to see that apart from mounds of silk cushions there were also chairs on which to sit, but decided not to occupy one of them until Mr. Khan arrived. If he sat on a cushion, she would do the same.

Her nervousness increased, and she looked round to ask the servant if she would have to wait long. But he had gone and, afraid that if she just stood here she would become even more nervous, she focused her attention upon her surroundings, noting the high, domed ceiling inlaid with arabesques in yellow, aubergine, and lapis blue upon a white marble ground. The same white marble had been used for the walls though those were interspersed with panels of pure mosaic, their prevailing color once more lapis lazuli.

"Miss Peters?" A mellifluous voice made her spin round, and she hoped the distance of the room had hidden her start of surprise as she caught her first sight of her host. He was far younger than she imagined—somewhere in his thirties—and she could not understand why Madame Nadar had said he was old. But as he came towards her and the clear white light of the room illumined his face, she knew that unless he had married in his early teens he could not possibly be Nizea's father.

"I am Karim Khan," he stated. "My father begs you to excuse him, but he is indisposed and unable to see you today." Color came into her cheeks, giving them an apricot bloom, and he was quick to see it. "He went riding yesterday and is now paying the penalty with a severe attack of lumbago."

The thought of the lofty Ibrahim Khan being laid low by so plebeian a malady made her want to smile, and she bit her lip hard in order to prevent it.

"My father has asked me to see you instead," the younger man continued and motioned her to sit down.

She hesitated, waiting to see where he was going to sit and, as she made no move, neither did he, and they stood looking at each other.

"Are you going to sit on a chair or a cushion?" she asked finally, her voice breathless.

"Will it make any difference?"

"I would feel foolish sitting above you."

"I would not be worried by a woman's looking down upon me," he said with a vestige of a smile; then, to her relief, he seated himself gracefully in a chair.

He wore a faultlessly cut charcoal gray suit. It looked lighter because of the honey gold color of his skin which, despite the intense black of his hair and eyebrows, had a smooth velvety quality unusual in a man. It would have been hard to believe he needed to shave had she not seen the faint shadow along his lower cheeks and chin. A firm nose divided a face that would have been happily accepted by any film star, though there was something brutal about his mouth, with its narrow upper lip and sensual lower one. The same hint of savagery was echoed by the square chin and heavy-lidded eyes. It was the eyes, Fleur thought nervously, that made him look so fierce, for they were those of a hawk and had the same intensely piercing stare.

"I believe you wished to talk to my father about my sister?"

The man moved his head slightly, and his hair caught the light. It was the thickest, shiniest hair she had seen, and it grew well down the nape of his neck and around his ears, ending in longish sideburns. Give him a moustache and put him in a turban, and he could well have sat for a portrait of a Mogul Emperor.

"Well?" he added sharply, and she quickly brought her mind back to the present and saw that although he was leaning indolently back in his chair, his expression was one of impatience.

"I wanted to talk about Nizea's future," she said nervously. "I am very concerned that she—that she should take advantage of her ability."

"We, too, are concerned on this account. She is seventeen and already a woman."

"Yes, well . . ." Fleur felt her cheeks growing warm. "I wasn't thinking of your sister in quite that way. I mean I'm not concerned with your plans for her marriage or anything like that."

"Naturally not. That is a matter for her family."

He looked so haughty that her nervousness began to be replaced by faint anger. Did he have to look at her in such a supercilious way and make it so obvious she should be impressed because he was sparing her his valuable time?"

"I came here to talk about Nizea's future education," she went on firmly. "I don't know whether you are aware of it, Mr. Khan, but she is a very talented girl and an able writer."

"She has always had a vivid imagination."

He made it sound like an insult, and Fleur's anger grew. "She has more than imagination, Mr. Kahn. She has a genuine gift. I think it should be encouraged."

"Encouraged?"

"She should go to the university. I am sure she would have no trouble in passing her entrance examination. She is one of my best pupils."

There was silence. The man half turned his head and appeared to be studying the wall some distance away. It gave him an even more remote look and increased his air of indifference.

"We are delighted that Nizea is showing attention to her studies," he said finally. "Until you came on the scene, she was more anxious to leave school than to remain there. This idea of going to the university—it is something you have put in her mind?"

"Certainly not." Fleur's softly rounded chin looked firmer as she tilted her head. But she found it hard to look into the heavy-lidded eyes that had suddenly turned to look at her, feeling as though she were being impaled by a hawk. "Nizea herself wants to continue her studies. That's why she asked me to . . . That's why I'm here. To plead her case."

"You are a charming advocate, Miss Peters." The deep voice was more gentle now. "However, my sister's future is already decided. She will leave school at the end of this term and will start to prepare for her wedding. Her future husband has already waited more than a year and does not wish to wait any longer."

"But Nizea doesn't want to get married!"

"I was not aware that the teachers at Madame Nadar's school interfered in the private lives of their pupils."

"Teachers should be able to talk to their pupils about everything that matters to them."

"Not the teachers in *our* country, Miss Peters. That is what the family is for. We do not abdicate our responsibilities to strangers, the way you so frequently do in the West."

Accepting the futility of arguing this point, she concentrated on the main one. "But Nizea is still a child."

The momentary lifting and lowering of his lids showed he was quick to see the implied criticism, though when he spoke his voice was still gentle. "In the East our women mature at an earlier age."

"But Nizea hasn't. She doesn't want to get married. She wants to go to the university. She wants to go on learning."

"Her husband will teach her."

"I'm talking about education. Not the sort of things that . . . that a man can teach her."

"Obviously; and that is where we fail to find common ground."

He rose, tall and lithe, towering above her in a way that few Persian men did. Again she was reminded of the Mogul Emperors of the past, the benevolent despots who had once ruled so much of Asia.

"You have a Western woman's appreciation of what

the female requires," he went on. "And it is not applicable to the women here."

"I don't agree with you."

She stood up, feeling at a disadvantage because she had to tilt her head back in order to look at him. She judged him to be several inches over six feet, with broad shoulders tapering to a narrow waist, and the long lean hips of a horseman. It was easy to imagine him riding across the desert on a stallion whose gleaming coat was no less black than the hair of its master, and whose rippling flanks were but an echo of the muscles hidden in the chest and thighs of the man who rode him.

Hurriedly she controlled her thoughts, angry at being trapped by the virile strength he exuded. It was as if he were subconsciously telling her that women were only creatures with whom a man dallied for sensual pleasure. For the more serious things in life, one did not bother with them.

"I was under the impression," she said in a trembling voice, "that in modern Iran women were allowed to benefit from education, and that if they had the capabilities they were encouraged to go to the university. Your country is still concerned with illiteracy, and many of your young people spend a period of national service teaching primary education and hygiene in the outlying villages."

"That is true. But my sister will not be doing this form of national service. She will be married instead."

"But she doesn't want to be married! If she did, she wouldn't have asked me to come here and talk to her father."

The man was silent, rubbing at his cheek with one long, supple finger. "My sister is fond of you—and having met you, I can see why. You have culture and intelligence, which one would expect from a woman of your class and country. Because of that, Nizea has tried to be what she knows you would like her to be."

"Your sister isn't pretending with me," Fleur interrupted. "She feels so deeply about it that she has even threatened to kill herself rather than marry a man she doesn't love!"

The features in front of her grew rigid with rage, and the heavy lids lifted to give her the full battery of a hard black stare. "My sister knows better than to blackmail *me* with threats like that. But she undoubtedly knows the best way of gaining *your* sympathy. It is unwise to be too tenderhearted with her, or she will take advantage of you."

"Nizea is the one of whom advantage is being taken," Fleur said icily. "Because she is a girl, you believe you can ride roughshod over her feelings."

"We understand Nizea's feelings better than you do, Miss Peters. She is a highly strung, overimaginative girl."

"She is also highly intelligent. It would be criminal to put her into purdah!"

For the first time he smiled. It was a wide, uninhibited movement of his mouth and disclosed perfectly formed white teeth. It also made him look far younger than she had judged him to be. If he had come in smiling, she would have put him at no more than twenty-eight.

"I hope your knowledge of English literature is better than your knowledge of modern-day Iran," he said in amusement. "It is many years since our women were kept in purdah. I know you think we are trying to curtail Nizea's freedom, but I can assure you it is merely a family's desire to protect its youngest member. My sister is, as you say, intelligent and with some talent, and this makes it all the more necessary for her to be controlled."

"She's a woman—not a horse!" Fleur's eyes sparked with anger, heightening the green in them. "How would *you* have reacted if you had not been allowed to follow your own choice of career?"

"I cannot answer emotional suppositions. I wanted to be a lawyer, and my father was fully in agreement."

"You are a lawyer?" She could not hide her surprise. "Then you of all people should value a person's rights!"

"I do." He flicked an imaginary speck of dust from his sleeve. The movement showed the muscles on his broad chest, and again he was reminded of a high-bred stallion. "If I were allowed to make my own decision about my sister's future, I would not be averse to letting her continue her education."

"Then why . . . ?"

"Because I am only Nizea's brother, and our father has decreed otherwise."

"Have you never disobeyed him?"

"For myself I might consider doing so," he replied, "but I would never encourage anyone else to do the same."

'I am surprised by your attitude, Mr. Khan. I judged you to be a man of conviction." The flash in his eyes told her she had insulted him, and the color in her cheeks deepened. "Forgive me. I . . . I didn't mean it the way it sounded."

"You should guard your tongue with the same care that we like to guard our women," he said coldly. "Then it would be in no danger."

The warmth in her cheeks spread to the rest of her

body, and she was glad she was wearing a high necked dress. It was clear there was no point continuing the conversation, and she moved to the door.

"You will take tea."

It was a statement, not a question, and, remembering the wording of the letter, she was embarrassed.

"Your rudeness to me," he went on, "does not absolve me from my duty as a host."

"I thought we had finished our discussion."

"We will talk of other things," he said, and paused as two women servants came in.

One had a silk cloth over her arm and was about to spread it upon a Persian rug on the floor when the man spoke to her in sibilant tones. She immediately set the cloth upon one of the mother-of-pearl-inlaid tables, and the second servant placed several dishes of sweetmeats upon it. As she was doing this, the first one went out and returned carrying a silver tray and a silver-and-gold tea service. While this was being arranged on the table, a small bowl filled with lemon scented water was held in front of Fleur, who knew enough of Persian customs to dip her fingers in it and wipe them on the warm towel held out for her.

As silently as they had come in the two girls glided out. They wore white muslin blouses and long tight black trousers with short, blue net overskirts that resembled the tutu of a ballerina. She dragged her eyes away from the fascinating picture they made and found her host regarding her.

"You are intrigued by their costumes?"

"Yes." It was good to get on to an impersonal subject. "They are most unusual."

"They were designed many years ago by one of our rulers. He was a guest of your Queen Victoria and visited the famous Alhambra Theatre. He was intrigued by the costumes he saw there, and when he returned to Persia, he designed something similar."

A servant girl returned and began to pour the tea into fragile gold-and-blue cups. The tea itself was fragrant, and though milk was offered, Fleur declined it. She would have liked to decline the sweetmeats but, knowing it would be impolite to refuse, she took the first one that came to hand. It looked like a meringue but tasted of ground almonds and was so light it melted in her mouth. Another one was immediately offered, but she shook her head and instead sipped her tea.

Karim Khan had seated himself in a chair again. He declined the sweetmeats with an imperious wave of his hand but drank his tea quickly.

"Do you like my country?" he asked unexpectedly.

"I haven't seen very much of it yet," she said politely. "But I like Teheran."

"What brought you to Madame Nadar's school? It is not the sort of place I would have expected to find you."

"I taught at a British boarding school." Her green eyes glinted. "Cold baths and hockey is much more my métier, I suppose."

He refused to be baited. "You answered an advertisement?"

"No, Mr. Khan. A friend of mine works here and, when he heard of the vacancy, he suggested I should apply for it."

"A Persian friend of yours?"

She shook her head. "An Englishman—Rory Baines. He works in the legal department of an oil company."

"Did your parents not object to your living thousands of miles away from home?"

"Why should they? I'm not a child."

"But you are a woman." He heard her exclamation, and his mouth curved upwards slightly. "It is surely normal for parents to worry more about the safety of their daughters than about their sons?"

"My parents didn't think I was coming to live in the wilderness," she said evenly.

The inclination of his head signified that he took her point. At the same time, he set down his cup with a finality that told her he was anxious to go. Quickly she set down her own cup and rose.

"Thank you for your hospitality, Mr. Khan. It was kind of you to spare me your time."

"How beautifully you tell your social lie."

His smile came again, but she did not return it. Nor did she hold out her hand, uncertain if it was expected of her. But as she turned to leave she found him beside her, and he walked with her from the room and across the large, cool hall with its high, domed ceiling to the inner courtyard. He paused there and while she was again debating whether to hold out her hand, she found it clasped briefly.

"My servant will see you out, Miss Peters. And please, I beg you not to think too harshly of us. My father wants what is best for Nizea's happiness."

Not even politeness could make Fleur concede this, and she remained rigid, only moving as she felt the servant at her elbow.

"Good-bye, Mr. Khan," she said and walked past the fountain to the smaller, outer courtyard.

Unwilling to walk through the streets, she was on the point of asking for a taxi to be called for her when a black Cadillac came through the outer gates and stopped in front of her. The servant opened the rear door and tentatively she got in. She had not expected to be provided with a car to take her home and would have given much to know if the arrangement had been made before her arrival. It was unlikely that after her sharp exchange with the son of the house he would have thought to do it. He was more likely to have wanted to string her up by her hair!

It was amazing that a man of education and obvious intelligence should have such old-fashioned views regarding his sister. Heaven help his poor wife! She tried to conjure up a picture of the woman but could see only a colorfully dressed serving girl. That would be much more the sort of creature he would have around him: a docile, subjugated female who looked on him as her lord and master.

Three

"IT was as I expected," Madame Nadar commented after hearing Fleur's account of her meeting with Karim Khan. "Now perhaps you will be content to let the matter rest and not encourage Nizea in her dream."

"Why should it be a dream? Prejudice is the only thing stopping her from doing what she wants."

"You would be wise to recognize its force and not fight it."

"I can't understand her brother's thinking the way he does. After all, he's an educated man."

"Education has nothing to do with one's emotion. He may have accepted many Western customs, but that doesn't mean he has discarded his own."

Fleur nodded and thought of the lordly way he had let the servants wait on him. "I'm just so sorry for Nizea."

"You must temper your sympathy with tact," Madame Nadar warned. "It would be bad if my school got the reputation of encouraging insurgence. Parents send their daughters here to be educated—not indoctrinated!"

"I'd hardly call it indoctrinating them to teach them some degree of independence."

"Our girls are not encouraged to be independent."

There was a note of warning in Madame's voice that told Fleur she would be unwise to argue further. She had come here on a year's contract, it was true, but Madame could no doubt find a way of terminating it before then if she wished.

"I've no intention of fighting Mr. Khan," Fleur stated. "Red-haired though I am, I'm not quite so foolhardy!"

Madame smiled. "I'm glad to hear it. It is far more intelligent to give in to the inevitable."

Rory Baines echoed this sentiment when he took Fleur to dinner a few nights later on his return from London.

"If I had been here before you wrote that letter, I'd have told you not to waste your time," he said. "Old man Khan is a real despot."

"So is his son."

"I've never met him. But he's got a formidable reputation as a lawyer. Several big American firms have been angling for him. Some British ones, too."

"I'm sure no money was spared on *his* education," Fleur said bitterly.

"He's Khan's only son."

"And daughters don't count?"

"Not in the same way." Rory leaned toward her. "*You* count though, my little firebird. I couldn't get you out of my mind while I was away. Did you miss me when I was in London?"

"I was too busy working to miss you." She saw his smile fade and added quickly, "I put in awfully long hours."

"Don't do more than you're paid for," he said. "Madame Nadar won't have any scruples about using you."

'Women are accustomed to being used," Fleur retorted. "Men have been doing it for centuries!"

Rory laughed, his thin, freckled face creasing into many lines. He was an unassuming looking man with a warm personality that made him attractive to women. Average in height, with fairish hair and soft brown eyes, he used his seeming mediocrity as a cloak to hide a mind that was both quick and subtle. Fleur had known him for a year and, though he had asked her to marry him six months after they met, she had been too unsure of her own feelings to say yes. Shortly afterwards, he had left for Iran and they had corresponded regularly, her liking for him deepening during his absence so that she had half regretted turning him down. When he had written and told her there was a teaching post available for her in Teheran, she had unhesitatingly accepted it, knowing it would give her a chance to reassess her feeling toward him and also see something of the world.

Within a month of being with him again, she had known she could never regard him as more than a friend, though having come thousands of miles to work near him, it was difficult to make him accept this.

"How was your trip to London?" she asked.

"Cold and damp but successful. I'll give it another year

here—maybe less—then I'll make tracks for home. I'd like to get out of oil and into proper legal work again."

"I hope you won't leave before I do," she said lightly. "I'd feel lost without you."

"Maybe I should let you feel lost. It might make you realize how important I am in your life."

"I don't need to miss you to know that," she smiled. "But it doesn't mean I love you."

"How can you be sure if you don't give yourself a chance to find out? I wish you'd come away with me." She shook her head and he sighed heavily. "You're so beautiful and sophisticated, I can't believe you're as old-fashioned as you act."

"It isn't an act."

"You're an anachronism then. Maybe that's why you came to Iran!"

"Oh, no," she laughed. "Compared with Persian women I'm totally liberated."

"Which reminds me," Rory said, refilling her wine glass. "How did the Khan girl take her family's refusal to do as you asked?"

"In a surprisingly subdued manner. I expected an explosion but it didn't come."

"Don't encourage one," he warned, "or you'll end up in the middle of a family feud and have your ears cut off!"

"I can imagine the Khans doing it too." She shivered. "Let's not talk about them any more."

"Good idea." He looked around for the waiter. "I'll settle up and we'll go on somewhere and dance."

They invariably did this when they went out and usually ended up with the American and European crowd with whom he worked. He was an extrovert and liked to

show her off—a fact which always embarrassed her—
though tonight she was glad of his wholehearted admiration, so different from the obvious disapproval that had
emanated from Karim Khan. She tried to envisage the
aloof Persian living in America and England, where he
had obtained his degrees, but could not see him fitting
into either country. He was too exotic a bird to be happy
in anyone else's territory.

The following day Nizea did not come to school, and
Fleur was dismayed to learn that the girl had fallen down
a flight of stairs and broken her leg.

"She is in the hospital," Madame Nadar informed her,
"and is unlikely to be back for the rest of the term."

"That means she won't be able to sit for her university
entrance," Fleur said in dismay.

"As she won't be going to the university . . ."

"I still wanted her to take it and see how she did."

"If she had passed, it would have made her more dis-
contented. It's far better that she doesn't take it."

"Do I have your permission to send her a couple of
novels as a gift?"

"You don't need my permission to send one of your
pupils a present."

"I realize that, Madame, but as it's Nizea . . ."

Madame nodded to show her appreciation of Fleur's
tact, though she might not have been so appreciative had
she seen her young teacher's choice of books: a Saul Bel-
low, a Lawrence Durrell, and a haunting but tender story
of life in a Yorkshire mining town during the depression
of the 1930s.

Another week went by, and Teheran became less cold.
The Judas trees were in bloom, and the flowerbeds in the

garden around the school were full of pansies. The silver plane trees were no longer leafless but wore their new green skirts and seemed as integral a part of the capital as the chestnut trees do in Paris.

As the Persian New Year approached, everyone began to make plans for ways of spending the holiday. All Persians were expected to spend the day fasting near running water, though the Europeans merely headed for the hills with picnic baskets.

Rory took it for granted that she would spend the day with him and, since the school was closed, she could not find an excuse to refuse his offer of a weekend at the house of some friends who lived in the mountains outside the capital. She still found it strange that the Persian weekend should cover Thursday and Friday instead of Saturday and Sunday but, since the Muslims' sabbath day was Friday, it was logical from their point of view.

It was the first time Fleur had gone out of the city, and she looked forward to seeing something of the landscape. She had been told that parts of it were like Spain but found the resemblance only superficial. The rocky hills were interspersed with areas of thick trees, more jungle-like than one would ever find south of the Pyrenees.

Her host and hostess were an American couple in their midthirties who took it for granted that she and Rory were more than friends. There was a moment of embarrassment when Mary Jackson made it clear that she and her husband had no objection if they wished to share a room.

"Fleur isn't my girl friend," Rory said plaintively, "though it's not for want of trying."

Mary laughed but later told Fleur she thought Rory a darling man whom most girls would be delighted to have.

It made Fleur see her behavior toward him as selfish. If she did not love him, it would be kinder not to monopolize his time. By continuing to see him, she was letting him believe something meaningful might yet develop.

Because of this she hedged when, the weekend over and she was saying good-bye to him outside Madame Nadar's house, he asked when he could see her again.

"The senior girls are taking their exams in a few weeks, and there's a lot of cramming to be done."

"You surely won't be working every single night?"

"Possibly not, but I won't know which ones I'll have free."

"*I* can be free any time," he said meaningfully. "When you find you can get away for a couple of hours, let me know."

"I will," she said, with no intention of doing so and allowed him to kiss her briefly before saying good-night.

If she went on seeing him, it would be easy to make herself believe she liked him enough to be serious about him, but there was no feeling of enchantment—which she had always assumed would exist between herself and the man she would love. Was she being overromantic to think this way? Would she be wiser to settle for companionship and understanding? After all, she and Rory liked the same things and held the same beliefs—unlike Karim Khan who did not believe in anything she held dear. Angry that the Persian should come into her mind, she tried to push him out of it. But he remained there like some elusive spirit, tantalizing her with his all-knowing smile and heavy-lidded eyes.

Hardly had Fleur finished her breakfast the next morning when she was asked to go to Madame Nadar's office.

"I had intended to speak to you last night," the woman said after she had inquired whether Fleur had enjoyed her weekend, "but you came back later than I expected and I was already asleep."

"Is anything wrong?" Fleur asked.

"No, no. I only wanted to tell you I had made arrangements for you to give Nizea private tutoring. The child has been brought home and is fretting at not being able to take her examination. Mr. Khan telephoned me during the weekend and asked if it were possible for you to visit her each day."

"How can I?" Fleur was dismayed. "What about my class? I've nineteen other girls to teach. I can't let them down because of one."

"I was not suggesting you let them down." Madame looked dutifully horrified. "I was hoping that for the next few weeks you would be willing to teach Nizea in the late afternoon, when school is over. I know it will mean a long day for you, but it will be for only a month."

Fleur bit her lip. When she had told Rory she would be working every night, she had not realized her lie would come true. That would teach her to tempt Fate. Hard on this thought came another. If she went to Nizea's home, she might have to see Nizea's brother. It was not a prospect she relished, and she looked so disturbed that Madame gave a gusty sigh.

"I cannot force you to go if you are reluctant. I pay you only to teach here."

"It has nothing to do with money," Fleur said at once.

"But it would mean working long hours and, if I were tired, I wouldn't be capable of doing my job."

"I think two hours a day with Nizea would be more than enough. And we can rearrange your hours here so that you can leave by three each afternoon."

"You're making it difficult for me to refuse," Fleur sighed.

"And if you refuse, you would make it difficult for *me*." The woman rested her pudgy hands on the desk. She was big and plump, with hair that grew well down over her forehead, giving her a simian look. "I owe a debt of gratitude to Mr. Khan. When I found myself widowed and had to return here, he generously loaned me the money to open this school. I have paid him back long since, but I have never forgotten his kindness."

"In that case I cannot refuse to do as you ask."

Madame Nadar smiled. "I am glad you understand my predicament."

Fleur was at the door when she remembered something else. "If Mr. Kahn doesn't want his daughter to go to the university, why does he want her to take the examination?"

"I believe his son persuaded him."

As she walked to her class, Fleur puzzled over the younger man's behavior. From his attitude when they had met, she would have expected him to oppose any further education for his sister.

Madame Nadar kept her word, and Fleur's classes were rearranged to let her leave school at three o'clock that afternoon. She had no time to change but wore one of the dark cotton shirtwaisters in which she normally taught. The one today was in deep blue with a wide belt that

showed her twenty-three-inch waist to advantage. Despite
her low heels, she was still much taller than the average
Persian woman—and more colorful looking, too, she
thought, running a comb through the red-gold waves that
fell to her shoulders. Muttering, she pinned back her hair
in a severe French pleat and hid her sparkling green eyes
behind dark glasses. Although it was spring and not hot,
the sun had a bright intensity rarely found in England at
this time of the year.

It was not until she went downstairs to ask a servant to
get her a taxi that she discovered the Khans had thought-
fully sent a car for her. It was the same limousine that
had brought her home a couple of weeks earlier, and she
sat in the back with a sense of familiarity. She had never
anticipated returning to Karim Khan's house. But it was
not his house; it was his father's. If she remembered that,
she wouldn't feel so on edge at the prospect of going
there.

Fleur's fear of meeting the younger man made her ap-
prehensive for the first few days. But when a week went
by without his putting in an appearance, she concluded he
did not come home until after she had left the house or, if
he did, that he was careful to keep out of her way.

Nizea was restless at being confined to bed but otherwise was a model pupil. With no other girl to take Fleur's
attention away from her, she proved to be a highly responsive student and, in a few hours, would do as much
work as if she had been at school all day.

On Wednesday, Fleur met Nizea's mother. She was an
older edition of her daughter and looked far too young to
have a son of Karim's age. She did not make much conversation and spoke poor English though excellent

French. She would drift into her daughter's room, listen for a few moments to the lesson, and then glide out again, leaving behind a flowery scent that took several hours to evaporate.

"My mother cannot understand why I do not wish to live the kind of life she does," Nizea grumbled on one occasion. "But she is so easily pleased and never gets bored doing nothing."

"Running this house can't be called doing nothing."

The girl burst out laughing. "My mother doesn't run the house. Aunt Maideh does. She's my father's sister, and she's lived with us all her life. My grandparents died when my father was very young, and he took care of all his brothers and sisters."

"That's one of the nicest things about your way of life," Fleur said. "The way you take care of your relations and don't abandon old people."

"We care more about old people than we do about the young," Nizea muttered bitterly. "I'm not allowed to have any opinions of my own, and I'm always expected to obey my elders."

"Young people all the world over say that," Fleur grinned. "So don't pity yourself by thinking you're the only one."

"I never pity myself," Nizea said with spirit. "I'm too busy thinking up ways of making my father change his mind about me. I am going to go to the university," she added darkly.

"You would be wiser to forget it," Fleur warned.

"Never."

Reluctant to get involved in another argument, Fleur stood up to go. To her surprise Nizea begged her to remain for dinner, pleading loneliness as her reason, and concluding with the sly comment that they served far better food that Madame Nadar.

"But I'll feel in the way," Fleur protested. "Your parents . . ."

"They'll be delighted to know you're keeping me company."

Fleur accepted the invitation and thoroughly enjoyed the excellent dinner served to them on a trolley. It seemed ungracious to leave immediately afterwards, and it was nearly nine before she bade her pupil good-night.

The following day Nizea took it for granted she would stay that night as well. "Time goes so much more quickly when you're here to talk to me, and if I'm left alone I get miserable and send my temperature up."

"You haven't had a temperature for days," Fleur teased.

"I'll get one if you leave! Besides, even though you're English and don't consider food important, you can't tell me you prefer to have dinner at school?"

"Like George Washington, I cannot tell a lie," Fleur laughed. "But I can't dine here on a regular basis."

"Of course, you can. You will be doing my family a favor."

By the time dinner was over it was usually after nine, and Fleur would hurry to the waiting car that took her through the brightly lit streets of Teheran to the quiet suburb which was now her temporary home.

"You should not allow Nizea to commandeer so much of your time," Madame Nadar commented one afternoon as Fleur was leaving for her daily visit. "I hadn't realized you would be staying there so late each evening."

"Nor had I," Fleur admitted. "But it's pointless making an issue of it now. In another ten days Nizea will be taking her exam, and I'll be free."

"How is her leg healing?"

"It's still in plaster, and I know she's often in pain. I try not to talk to her about it because she likes to dramatize it."

She remembered this when she entered the girl's room half an hour later and found her weeping and banging her head on the side of her bed.

"I can't take the examination, Miss Peters. All the work we've done has been for nothing."

"What do you mean? I thought your father . . ."

"It has nothing to do with my father. It's the doctor. He isn't satisfied with the way my leg is healing and says I must go into the hospital again."

"You poor child." Sympathy brought Fleur to the bedside. "I'm sure it's all for the best. You've been feeling far more pain than you should have done. You must at least be grateful that the doctor has discovered there's something wrong which he can put right."

"They should have put it right the first time they operated," Nizea cried.

"These things sometimes happen," Fleur placated.

"My father doesn't think so. I heard him tell Mama he's bringing in another surgeon from Paris. He arrives tomorrow morning."

Fleur marveled at the speed and ease with which things could be done when there was sufficient money at one's disposal. But in order to benefit from such a moneyed world, Nizea also had to be controlled by it.

"You'll still come and see me each day, won't you?" the girl pleaded, holding Fleur's hand.

"If I'm allowed to be with you, I'll be there," Fleur promised.

"Why shouldn't you be allowed? I'm only having my leg reset. In a couple of days I'll be quite well enough to study."

"Is it Miss Peters' teaching that you enjoy so much, or is it her company?"

The deep voice that spoke from the doorway made Fleur turn, and it required no introduction to tell her she was facing the master of the house.

A tremor weakened her legs and for no logical reason her heart started to pound. Staring into the dark eyes she had a premonition that this man was going to be important in her life; that his wishes and commands would affect her behavior and her happiness. It was a ludicrous thought and she tried to dismiss it. Their worlds were so far apart that what she did could have no significance for him. Certainly what *he* did would mean nothing to *her*. But the uneasiness persisted, folding itself around her like a shroud so that she wanted to shake herself free of it.

But was it Ibrahim Khan who frightened her or the authority he represented? Deciding it was a little of both, she also accepted the fact that as long as she remained in Persia she would consciously resist the subtle pressures of male dominance.

Ibrahim Khan's hooded eyes were impassive as they met her own; then a flicker appeared in their depths, almost as if her thoughts had become visible and he was reading them. She had had the same impression when she had met his son.

I'm being fanciful, she admonished herself. *As far as he's concerned I'm an insipid little English teacher whom he can dismiss any time he wants. And he'll have no hesitation in doing it if he ever thinks I'm trying to lessen his authority.*

Four

WITH firm strides Ibrahim Khan came farther into the room. If his son had made her think of a hawk, the father made her think of an eagle; proud, strong, king of the sky as the lion was king of the earth. Despite his European clothes he looked so Middle Eastern that he might just as well have worn a flowing burnoose. It was all very well for the Persians to say they were not Arabs, yet this man looked as if the desert was his natural habitat and that he could more easily ride a stallion than in an automobile.

He was considerably older than she had expected, though his air of command told her that only death would take the reins of control from his hands. His skin was swarthy and looked darker because of the heavy black beard that covered the lower portion of his face, masking his chin and almost hiding the thin-lipped mouth. He had the same dominant nose as his son, but his eyes were smaller and set below thick, bushy eyebrows. Age had not robbed him of his hair though it had put silver strands among the black, and he wore it brushed away from his high forehead, its fullness making it rise to a crest. Here was a man whose word was law and who would accept nothing less than total obedience. Remembering the letter she had written to him, Fleur wondered how she could have been so foolish. Nothing she could say would ever make him change his mind. There was no need to ask from whom his son had inherited his obstinacy.

"Please forgive me for not having met you earlier," Ibrahim Khan said, "but I too have been indisposed."

"So I understand," Fleur murmured. "Lumbago can be most unpleasant."

"It attacks without regard for age or rank." His smile gave a fierce charm to his face. "I wish to thank you for your kindness and patience with my daughter. She can be a great trial."

"Oh, Papa," Nizea pouted. "What an unfair thing to say."

"The truth is never unfair," came the admonition. "You rail against Fate, and you consider obedience an ugly word."

"Most teenagers are the same," Fleur put in hastily. "Nizea is much better than some other pupils I've had. Nor has she let her accident prevent her from working hard on her studies."

"All of which is unnecessary," the man stated firmly. "A year from now, and her examinations will mean nothing to her."

"That's not true!" his daughter cried angrily.

"It will become true. I have better judgment than *you* on this matter."

"But it's my life you're talking about!"

"I know what is best for you." The sharp black eyes moved to Fleur. "When I was young I would never have dared speak to my father the way I allow this child to speak to me."

"Times change," Fleur said gently.

"But certain things remain the same. Man has a great need to respect and look up to someone. He welcomes authority—be it from his father, his religion, or both. Give a man too much freedom and he will abuse it. He will destroy others and eventually end by destroying himself."

Fleur kept her eyes downcast. She was sure Ibrahim Khan was giving her a warning. Yet if he had had any doubts about her, surely he would not have allowed her to come here and teach his daughter?

"I appreciate your viewpoint, Mr. Khan, although it doesn't happen to be mine." She raised her head and looked at him, glad she could do so without fear. "Authority is good only as long as one doesn't become so dependent on it that one forgets how to use one's own mind."

The luxuriant beard moved slightly, as if the man was pressing his lips tightly together; then he moved closer to the bed and spoke to his daughter.

"I came in to tell you that Dr. Dubois has already left Paris and will be here to examine you first thing in the morning. It is likely he will operate later in the day. Dr. Mazda wished to take you into hospital tonight, but I thought you would be happier to remain at home for as long as possible."

"I would," Nizea said firmly.

"But no eating tomorrow, eh? And nothing this evening after midnight." He glanced over his shoulder at Fleur as he went to the door. "I bid you good-bye, Miss Peters, and thank you once again for your patience and kindness with my household."

Fleur acknowledged the words with a slight movement of her head, seeing them as a dismissal of her services. But she said nothing of this to Nizea when she was left alone with the girl, knowing that to do so would cause a storm of protest.

"Don't let's do any other lessons today," Nizea said. "Tell me about your British boarding school instead."

"I've already told you about it."

"Then tell me about your home. You sound as if you had a wonderful childhood."

Fleur almost said it had been idyllic compared with Nizea's, but knew that if the remark got back to Mr. Khan he was ruthless enough to use it to get her dismissed from Madame's school.

"Why don't *you* entertain me for a change?" she ventured. "Tell me about the Persian way of life—I find your customs and history far more fascinating than mine."

"No, they're not," Nizea grumbled.

"Yes, they are," Fleur insisted. "Your ancestors had a system of weights and measures and a detailed knowledge of astronomy when my ancestors were still painting themselves with woad!"

"You don't need me to tell you anything about Persian history," the girl giggled, her humor restored. "You know more about it than I do."

"I read a lot of books about it before I came here."

"Would you like to live here permanently?"

"Oh, no!" The words were said without thought, and Fleur colored. "The differences in our culture would make it difficult for me to put down my roots."

"What would happen if you fell in love with a Persian? Our men are very good-looking. Not like your pale, thin Englishmen!"

"They're not all pale and thin," Fleur protested. "Anyway, I think I'd find Persian men too overwhelming."

"They are also very demanding." It was a knowing remark, and made Nizea seem older than her age.

But Fleur was reluctant to let the conversation develop in case it gave the girl an opportunity to show her dissatisfaction with the life her father was planning for her.

"What d'you want to know about my childhood?" she asked quickly.

"Nothing until you answer the question I asked you. If you fell in love with a Persian, would you be able to let him be your master?"

"Providing he let me be his mistress," Fleur retorted, and then looked discomfited. "I didn't mean that the way it sounded."

"I should hope not!" Nizea giggled.

"What I mean is that I'd only be happy in a marriage where neither partner considered themselves to be in control of the other. A man and a woman should both have the same freedom to do what they think is right."

"You are talking of Western marriage."

"I'd prefer not to talk about marriage at all," Fleur said, "and it's naughty of you to try and force me to do so. You know very well your father is suspicious of my influence over you."

"He has no need to be. You are so careful what you say that I sometimes think you're more frightened of my father than I am!" The black eyes gleamed. "What d'you think of my brother? I bet he scares the wits out of you!"

"That will be quite enough, Nizea." Fleur remembered she was the teacher and drew herself up to her full height. "You are becoming overexcited, and it might be better if I left."

"Please don't go." The soft voice trembled. "I didn't mean to be rude. It's just that when we're away from school I can't think of you as my teacher. You're like one of my friends."

It was hard to resist such a compliment, though Fleur tried her best. "If you want me to stay with you, we must do some work."

"I wrote a story last night," Nizea said cautiously. "My leg was hurting me, and I couldn't sleep."

She drew a notebook from under her pillow, and Fleur took it to a chair by the window and began to read. By any standard it was an excellent story but, bearing in mind the youth and restricted life of the author, it showed an astonishing depth of perception. The main character depicted was that of an old man who, paralyzed by a stroke, was still determined to rule his family. He could not come to terms with the fact that he was unable to speak, nor would he accept that as far as the outside world was concerned, he was regarded as senile.

"You certainly have a vivid imagination," Fleur said, matter-of-factly when she came to the end. "Where did you get the idea for this story?"

"I was thinking of my father and how he would feel if he found he couldn't move or speak." The dark eyes were full of mischief. "I quite enjoyed thinking of Papa like that. I felt as if I was putting him in his place!"

"That's a dreadful thing to say." Fleur was genuinely shocked. "Your father wants what is best for you and . . ."

"What he believes to be best. That isn't the same thing. If you knew how unhappy I am . . ."

"I do know," Fleur cut in, "but I can't talk to you about it. I'm here to teach you, and I don't want to get involved in family matters."

Resolutely she refused to be sidetracked from the lessons they were supposed to be doing and, even when they relaxed during dinner, she was careful to let nothing personal creep into their conversation. If she had felt less deeply about her pupil's predicament, she might have been able to talk about it, but because she considered Mr. Khan almost criminal in his disregard of his daughter's talent—which this short story had further illustrated—she knew the only way she could maintain her neutrality was to ignore the subject entirely. It was a coward's way out but, as she wished to remain in Teheran for the length of her contract, she had no option.

At nine o'clock Nizea's nurse came in to settle her charge for the night, and Fleur felt free to go.

"Don't forget to come and see me in the hospital," Nizea reminded her.

"I'll come as soon as you're allowed visitors."

"I want you to be my first one. I wish I had a sister like you, Miss Peters."

Fleur smiled and thought of the problems she might have had with a sister as tempestuous as this one. Yet much of Nizea's unrest came from the stifling of her talent and would never have arisen had she been born into a Western family. It would be interesting to know where the girl's writing ability came from. She was so intrigued by this that she found herself in the main hall before she realized she was there. At night it was softly lit by colored glass lamps that stood on pedestals in the archways. The evening air was so still that the fountain in the inner courtyard could be heard playing as she slipped on her coat—for the nights were cool—and walked across to the lapis lazuli basin. In the moonlight it looked midnight blue. She raised her head and stared at the stars, thinking how clear they looked.

"You stayed too late with my sister."

With a violent start she turned round, wondering irritably whether the Khan men made a habit of appearing when they were least expected.

"Forgive me if I frightened you."

Karim Khan stepped forward from the shadows. He was in a dinner jacket, and a wide, deep blue cummerbund encircled his waist. It was an exotic touch that went well with his appearance.

"You should walk more loudly," she said. "Then you wouldn't take people by surprise."

"To walk with quietness has been bred in us," he replied. "But next time I approach you, I will cough." He came to stand by the edge of the fountain basin, a few feet away from her.

"Why didn't you leave earlier?" he asked.

"Nizea likes me to stay and keep her company."

"My mother would be happy to do that."

"I have no wish to usurp her place," Fleur said hastily.

"You could never do that."

She was glad the moonlight hid the color that rushed into her face, though her indrawn breath must have told him she hadn't liked his comment.

"It was a statement, Miss Peters, not a criticism. My mother cannot give Nizea what you give her—the stimulation of intellectual conversation."

"I'm surprised you think women need it!"

The flash of his teeth told her his lips had parted, though she was not sure whether in a smile or in annoyance. However, when he spoke there was irony in his soft voice.

"You seem determined to quarrel with my views about women."

"You are your father's son."

"And a dutiful one. That makes it hard for me to disobey him."

"Even if you considered he were wrong?"

"If you are referring to his attitude towards my sister's education, then I am by no means sure he is wrong. I only know that if I were in his place I would not do the same."

It was a fine distinction which she was quick to follow. "You mean you'd be willing to let her go to the university?"

"Yes. But that doesn't mean I would be right. My father thinks Nizea will benefit from an early marriage and a strong husband to control her."

Control, there was that word again; as if a woman were an animal.

"I can see I have annoyed you," he went on smoothly. "Like most educated women of the West, you make the mistake of thinking that in a matter of decades you can change patterns that have evolved over thousands of years."

"You still see a woman as a creature that a man can drag into his cave by her hair!"

"You are putting it too starkly. I merely wish to love and cherish the women in my life. I see it as my duty to provide for them and to protect them."

"You wish to treat them like dolls who will walk and talk and smile only at your command."

"You misjudge me," he said softly and kept pace with her as she started to walk towards the intricately carved gates that led to the outer courtyard where the Khans' limousine always waited to take her back to school.

"I believe a woman is as capable of learning as a man," he continued, "but I also believe her biological make-up is different and that this difference must be satisfied before anything else."

"If you only see women as childbearers . . ."

"It isn't the way *I* see them that matters," he interrupted. "It is the way they see themselves. Even those who renounce motherhood have to do so with vehemence—as if they are talking against their basic needs. The future of the human race lies with the woman, and if she abdicates her role we will cease to exist."

"Not all women wish to abdicate." Fleur quickened her pace. "I'm sure there are many who are happy to lead the same lives as their mothers. All I'm saying is that those who don't, shouldn't be made to feel guilty."

"Most of them make their own guilt," he stated, "because they know they're going against their natural desires."

"If you believe that," she said irritably, "our discussion is over."

"I believe that women—being women—want the best of both worlds!" His voice was heavy with irony. "Those who wish to lead a life of the mind also wish to lead a life of the body. They want to walk side by side with their man, but when it suits them they want to be carried!"

"And what about men?" Fleur said furiously. "One minute they're conquerors and the next they're little boys running back to their women to be cosseted."

"At least man doesn't deny the dual nature of his personality."

"Women don't want to deny it, either," she cried. "All they want is the chance to develop. But it's men like you who prevent them."

They reached the outer courtyard, and she neared the car.

"It's as well that we part here," she added, "otherwise we should quarrel."

"We're already quarreling," he smiled, "and I'm enjoying it. I am on my way out, and I will take you home."

"There's no need." She indicated the car.

Ignoring her reply, he spoke to the chauffeur who immediately switched on the engine and purred away, leaving Karim to cross to a low-slung, cream-colored roadster, its soft leather top up against the night air. He held open the passenger door, and Fleur slid in, tensing as he took his place next to her. The inside of the car was large yet he dominated it with his size and seemed to tower above her, his proud head almost touching the roof. Give him a beard and he would be even more fierce-looking than his father. She forced her gaze away from his hawklike profile and stared ahead.

Expecting him to drive as though he owned the road, she was agreeably surprised by his care and, glancing at him, saw he was totally relaxed in his seat.

"You know my sister is having another operation?" he said suddenly.

"Yes, your father told me."

"So you have finally met my father. I will not ask what you thought of him."

"I don't make quick judgments on anyone."

"Only on me."

Her fingers clenched around her handbag. "You're a—you are rather different, Mr. Khan. You seem to enjoy going out of your way to—to provoke people."

"To provoke *you*," he corrected calmly. "I think it's the best way of puncturing your guard."

"If you employ that method in your work, I'm not surprised you're so successful."

"So you know how successful I am, eh?" His glance at her was swift but all-embracing. "Are you guessing or have you been told?"

"Rory—Mr. Baines—mentioned it."

"Your English friend?"

"Yes."

"Did he also mention that I did part of my legal training in England?"

She heard the teasing in his voice and reacted to it. "I find it amusing that you can have had the benefit of a Western education without Western ideas rubbing off on you."

"Why is it considered such a good thing for Western

ideas to rub off on those who aren't Western? Personally, I think it would be far better if some of our Eastern ideas rubbed off the other way!"

She knew he was waiting for her to disagree, and an impish surge of mischief made her deliberately overreact in the opposite way.

"You're absolutely right, Mr. Khan. The West can learn a great deal from the East. Your way of taking care of your elderly; your devotion to your parents; your ability to do things slowly without rushing and spoiling them. All these are characteristics we would do well to acquire."

There was silence for a hundred yards or more before he spoke.

"You disarm me with your honesty, Miss Peters. I hope you mean what you say and aren't merely dissembling?"

"You're far too astute to be fooled by a woman!"

He chuckled. "The more astute a man believes himself to be, the more easily he can be undone!"

"That sounds like a wise Persian saying!"

"I'll see that it becomes one!" He leaned forward to peer through the windscreen, and she quickly gave him directions.

"I'm sure I've taken you out of your way."

"No matter. I wished to take you. I wanted an opportunity to thank you for your kindness to my sister. You've been with her every night and have had no life of your own for weeks."

"I enjoy her company, and I've had some wonderful dinners."

He stopped the car outside the school gate and turned to let his eyes roam over her slender figure. "I don't get the impression that food is all that important to you," he said drily. "You look as fragile as a leaf on a winter bough."

It was a lovely smile, and she made a note of it, hoping that if she kept the logical part of her mind working, the foolish, emotional part would not start her quivering at his nearness. She could not remember meeting a man who managed to be so gentle and yet so aggressively male at one and the same time.

"All my family are tall and slim," she said nervously. "But we are very strong."

"You don't look it. I watched you coming down the stairs and you seem exhausted."

"The days are rather long," she admitted. "Examinations begin next week and . . ."

"You don't mean you are teaching in school as well as being with my sister?"

"Of course. I'm only with Nizea from late in the afternoon."

"Until late at night," he added sharply. "Madame Nadar should know better than to make you work such hours."

"It is my own choice," Fleur lied. "My senior girls are the same age as Nizea and are taking the same examination. I cannot neglect them."

"I didn't realize you would be called upon to do double duty. I was under the impression Madame Nadar had other teachers in the school."

"She has. But I've taught the girls their curriculum, and I have to see them through it."

"Then it's a good thing the exam begins soon," he said

roughly. "Otherwise you'd be nothing more than bones and hair."

"A lot of hair," she said, trying to inject some humor into the situation but sorry the moment she had spoken, for his glance turned to the riotous curls and remained there.

"Right now," he said softly, "the only thing that glows about you is your hair." He pressed a switch on the dashboard and the interior of the car lightened. "I've never seen such a color. Pinky gold might be one way of describing it."

"So might carrots," she retorted and fumbled for the car door.

"That is one thing Western women would do well to learn," he said.

Not understanding him, she paused in surprise and glanced at him over her shoulder.

"How to accept a compliment," he explained, "without getting embarrassed and wanting to run away."

She was on the point of denying both accusations when she realized that was what she was doing and, biting her lip, she opened the door. As she stepped on to the pavement she found him beside her. Silently he walked with her to the gates and waited as she took a key from her handbag and unlocked them.

"Good-night, Miss Peters." He held out his hand, and reluctantly she put hers into it.

"Good-night, Mr. Khan. Thank you for bringing me home."

He waited as she slipped through the gates and re-locked them and did not move until she had reached the front door and opened that, too. As she closed it behind him she heard the purr of his car in the stillness of the night. He was a strange man, Karim Khan. Remembering her sharpness with him, she vowed that if she met him again she would be more polite. But cool with it. He was no doubt used to women falling over him, and she did not want to give him the impression that she would do the same.

Five

FLEUR found herself thinking of Nizea throughout the next day. Knowing the girl would not be having her operation until the afternoon, she did not call the hospital till evening, when she learned that Nizea was as well as could be expected and that inquiries about her should be made direct to the family.

There was none of the English habit of giving complete details about a patient to any Tom, Dick, or Harry who called—a practice which Fleur had always considered an infringement of one's privacy—but she was, nonetheless, reluctant to phone the Khan household, uncertain as to who would take her call. However, Madame Nadar saved her the trouble by calling her in to say she had already spoken to Mr. Khan who had told her his daughter had come through the operation successfully and that the prognosis was excellent for a complete recovery.

It was a relief to Fleur not to have to leave the school each day and she settled back into her old routine, though she knew this would end when her senior class sat for their examination, and the rest of the school did their usual end-of-term one.

On Saturday she telephoned the hospital and asked permission to see Nizea. She arrived there in the late afternoon with a bottle of English lavender water which she had obtained with great difficulty. It was hard to know what to get a girl who had everything, and her efforts to do so seemed justified when she entered her pupil's room and found it awash with flowers and fruit. The girl looked wan, with an unbecoming sallowness, but she was in high spirits and thanked Fleur brightly for the scent, which she splashed all over her arms immediately, at the same time begging to be regaled with all the gossip from the school.

"I won't be able to take the examination on Monday," she confided, "but Karim has told me not to worry. He says he'll manage something for me."

Fleur did not know what the man had meant by this and diplomatically kept silent. "How long will you have to stay in the hospital?" she asked.

"I'm not sure. But when I come out we will be leaving Teheran to stay in our summer house."

"When somebody uses the word 'summerhouse' in England," Fleur smiled, "they mean a conservatory or a greenhouse."

Nizea giggled. "You could never describe *our* summer house that way. It's beautiful, Miss Peters. I'd love to show it to you. I think . . ." Her lips parted as if she had something more to say, but she averted her face and plucked at the counterpane covering her. "Several of the girls from school have been to stay there with me," she continued, "but I find them childish and boring."

"Some of them probably would be. You are very mature for your age."

"That's what I feel," Nizea said candidly. "Yet I have not done anything more exciting than they have. I have never been abroad like lots of them."

"Maturity comes from within," Fleur explained. "You have a seeing eye."

"What does that mean?"

"It means you see beyond the surface to what lies below. Painters have a seeing eye—although they use it in a different way. So do composers. I'm putting it in simplistic terms, of course."

"You're explaining it in a way I can understand," Nizea said. "That is what makes you a good teacher."

"You're a very responsive pupil," Fleur replied. "That's why it's such a pleasure teaching you."

"Is it really, Miss Peters?" The girl smiled with delight, though her face instantly clouded over. "What's the use of having a gift if I'm not allowed to use it?"

"No one is stopping you from using it. As I once told you, getting a degree won't necessarily make you a better writer. You might learn much more about the world and human feelings by becoming a nurse or a social worker."

"You still need training for that," came the sharp retort. "And my father is determined to marry me off within a year."

The girl lapsed into a moody silence, and Fleur tried to think of something to say that might make her less despondent. "You might find it easier to cajole your husband into letting you do what you want," she said casually. "Do you know the young man your father has in mind for you?"

"His name is Farouk Raj and he is the same age as Karim. He is rich and extremely well-connected. It is this last part that my father considers the most important, for we have more than enough money of our own." Her voice rose. "My friends think I'm mad because I don't want to marry him, but I can't bear the idea of being tied to *any* man."

Still Fleur held her tongue. It was a dreadful thing for Nizea to be married off to a man she did not love, but to agree with her would be courting disaster.

"How old is Mr. Raj?" she asked tentatively.

"Thirty-two. He and Karim celebrate their birthday within a week of each other, and they are good friends, too."

"I'm surprised your brother isn't married."

"So is my father." Nizea pulled a face. "He is always arguing with him because of it. You have no idea the number of girls my father has produced for his inspection. But he has turned them all down."

"Maybe he's looking for perfection." Fleur kept her voice expressionless, and Nizea gave her a suspicious look to see if she were being sarcastic. Then she decided to take the comment at face value.

"My brother is young, handsome, wealthy, and much respected. It would be a great honor to be his wife. He would also be an excellent lover."

"Nizea!" Fleur found it difficult to keep her face straight, for she · knew the Persian girl was deliberately teasing her. "You shouldn't say things like that."

"Why not? It's true. If I am considered old enough to

be married, then I'm old enough to know what marriage is all about."

"It's about more than sex," Fleur said positively.

"But sex is important." Nizea was equally as positive.

"I'm not denying its importance. I just think it should be seen in relationship to other things."

"How practical you sound," the younger girl laughed. "Yet I think that deep down you are a romantic."

"You know nothing of the way I feel."

"I know there is a man in love with you. Some of the girls who sleep at the school during the week have seen him when he's called for you. They say he's very English and not man enough for you."

"I don't wish to hear any more."

Fleur jumped up, aghast to think her affairs had been discussed at such length by a bevy of giggling schoolgirls. Rory not good enough for her? She caught sight of herself in the dressing-table mirror—slender as a wand in a cotton voile dress of ice-green, its bodice high-necked yet showing her full breasts and tiny waist, the circular skirt swinging upon her shapely calves. Impatiently she pushed away her hair from her face, pulling the heavy strands back behind her ears.

"I think we've talked enough for one afternoon, Nizea. I'm going to leave you to rest."

"But you've only arrived. You can't leave me yet."

There was a slight cough directly behind Fleur, and her scalp prickled, making it unnecessary for her to turn round to know who it was. That precise cough had made it all too clear.

"Good afternoon, Mr. Khan," she said coolly as he

came into her line of vision. "I'm glad you're here to keep your sister company. I'm just leaving."

"And preventing me from having the pleasure of driving you home?"

For an instant Fleur was flummoxed, then she found her tongue. "I'm returning to the school."

"No matter. I will take you where you wish to go. Please sit down."

His look defied her to disobey him and, because her knees were trembling, she did as he said, watching in silence as he greeted his sister with a playful touch on her shoulder, at the same time dropping a little package into her hand.

"For me," the girl exclaimed, and unwrapped it to show a gold bracelet laden with dangling charms. "Oh, Karim! It's exactly what I wanted. How did you know?"

"Because you've told me a hundred times in the past month!" he teased. "But if you lose this as quickly as you lost the other one, I won't replace it. So be warned."

He sauntered to the window and leaned against it. With the light behind him his shoulders looked broader and his hair more like black satin. His skin seemed more golden-brown too, and Fleur knew that before the summer was out it would become still darker. Even now it made him look fierce, and she lowered her head quickly before his piercing eyes could meet hers. Until now she had never considered herself susceptible to the way a man looked, but there was something about this one that made her vibrantly conscious of him. It was as if she were a microscope and able to see every detail about him. Without looking in his direction her brain enumerated them all: his elegantly curved eyebrows; the brilliance of his eyes with their intensely brown irises; the beautifully shaped mouth whose narrow upper lip was at variance with the sensuous lower one, and the firm chin with a cleft in the middle that robbed it of hardness. Again she knew him to be a man of contradiction; a man whom one could know a lifetime and never know at all.

"You seemed to be having an argument when I came into the room," he said to his sister, folding his arms across his chest. "I hope my arrival prevented a quarrel?"

"We weren't quarreling," Fleur intervened hurriedly.

"Miss Peters thought I was being rude about her personal life," Nizea added.

"Were you?"

"I didn't think so. But she is not used to the candor with which Persian women speak among themselves. Perhaps you can explain it for me."

"Do you think a man can explain the way women behave when they are together?"

"Not any man," his sister said, "but you can. I am sure you know how women behave at *all* times!"

"Take care," he mocked, "or you might be starting an argument with *me*."

The amusement in his voice made Fleur look at him. Expecting his gaze to be fixed upon his sister, she was disconcerted to find it resting on herself. Even across the width of the room she felt the power of his personality. She clasped her hands together, hoping he did not notice that they were trembling.

"What my sister wishes me to say to you, Miss Peters," he said, "is that our women regard the acquisition and retainment of a man as the most important thing in their life. Second to this is the importance they attach to helping other women—who don't have a man of their own—to acquire one. And since Nizea is already betrothed—albeit unwillingly—she feels she can safely turn her attention to *you*. I can assure you she had no intention of being rude and that her interest in your affairs stems only from the fact that she is your sincerest admirer."

Fleur went pink. "I wasn't really angry with Nizea, Mr. Khan. I was just a bit surprised by her candor."

"Because it came from a pupil?"

"Partly."

"Would you have minded if *I* had been as candid?"

"Probably more."

He threw back his head and laughed, a warm uninhibited sound that echoed around the room. As it died away he straightened and glanced at his watch. "I must leave now. I can drop you on your way, Miss Peters."

"Please don't bother."

His mouth thinned, as she knew it must have done the night she had encountered him in the courtyard and had refused his offer to take her home, only then it had been too dark for her to see it.

"I will take you," he repeated and waited while she collected her bag and bade Nizea good-bye.

In silence they went out to his car. It was the cream roadster again, but this time the top was down and he glanced at her briefly.

"Will the breeze spoil your hair?"

"It's naturally wavy. The breeze will only make it worse."

"Worse!" he said in bewilderment.

"Curlier," she explained.

"That would only make it more beautiful."

His hand half lifted and, afraid he was going to take a tendril, she drew back sharply. He saw the movement but made no comment as he opened the car door for her.

Soon they had left the modern hospital behind them and were driving along the broad, clean, white roads. It was early summer and already hot. Women in gay summer dresses walked with their menfolk, and groups of teenagers could be seen drinking coffee or fruit juices in the sidewalk cafés. It was only girls like Nizea, who came from rich, old-fashioned families, who were still forced to lead a secluded existence.

"Why the sigh?" the man beside her asked. "That's the second one in as many minutes."

"I was thinking of your sister," she admitted.

"Of what she said to you? I am curious to know exactly what it was."

"It was nothing really important." She dismissed this topic quickly. "I was thinking of her education. She let me read a short story of hers the other day, and it was a powerful piece of writing. Something I never expected from a seventeen-year-old."

He slowed the car but remained staring ahead, his lower lip jutting forward. "You genuinely believe she can write, don't you?"

"Of course. Why else do you think I pleaded for her?"

"I thought perhaps you were doing it because you were irritated by my father's old-fashioned attitude."

"That does irritate me," she said candidly, "but it would never make me exaggerate the gift your sister has. Have you never read any of her work?"

"Only the scribble she did as a child."

"You should read the story she gave me a couple of days ago."

"I will ask her for it."

Fleur stared through the side window, remembering Madame Nadar's injunction not to antagonize the Khan family, and hoping her suggestion would not cause an argument between father and son.

"You are still looking pale," he said suddenly. "I had hoped that with my sister in the hospital you would have had more time to yourself."

"Madame Nadar rarely allows one free time," Fleur smiled. "She has such enormous energy she can't see why anyone should get tired."

"Doesn't your contract stipulate your hours of work?"

"Yes, but . . ."

"Then you should stick to it."

"I'm quite happy as I am."

"But too pale," he reiterated. "Would you like me to have a word with her?"

Fleur was horrified, and he knew it at once. "I'm sorry, Miss Peters, that was a stupid thing for me to suggest. Of course I cannot talk to Madame Nadar without embarrassing you. But there may be another way."

"You must promise to say nothing," she said instantly. "Please, Mr. Khan, I mean it."

"Don't get so het up. I promise I'll keep quiet. There is more than one way of skinning a cat." He heard her chuckle and gave her a sidewise glance. "What have I said that amuses you?"

"The expressions you use. They're slangy and I didn't expect them from . . ." Her voice trailed away, but her embarrassment remained, increasing as she saw the sharp smile that momentarily moved his mouth.

"You see me as too Eastern to use Western slang?"

"Of course not. You speak perfect idiomatic English."

"Perfect idiomatic English," he repeated. "You sound very patronizing!"

"That was the last thing I intended," she said humbly. "I'm sorry, Mr. Khan. You have every right to be angry with me."

"I'm not angry with you, Miss Peters. And even if I had been, your apology would have caused it to disappear."

The hand nearest to her left the wheel and moved towards her. Then it stopped and clasped the wheel again. But she had the distinct impression that he had wanted to touch her, and she was glad to see they were approaching the school. As before, he was out of the car and by her side before she could reach the pavement, and he again watched while she unlocked the gate to let herself into the garden.

"You said you weren't going home," he reminded her, "but since you gave me no other address, I brought you here."

"I was going home," she confessed. "I only said I wasn't because . . . because I was embarrassed with you."

He gave her a hard stare through eyes so narrow that it was impossible for her to read their expression.

"I won't ask you why," he said abruptly and, without saying anything further, returned to his car and drove away.

With a disappointment that had no rhyme and reason,

Fleur let herself into the house. Normally she would have been pleased to have the rest of the day free, but now she regretted her refusal to go out with Rory and debated whether to call him and say she had changed her mind. Was her restlessness due to Nizea's unthinking prattle, or did it come from her conversation with Karim Khan? But she had only talked to him of trivialities, though he had a way of making even the trivial seem important. That was because he was so deliberate in everything he said, giving the impression that he gave great thought to all his statements. For a moment in the hospital she had almost believed he had come to see his sister because he had guessed that she herself would be there; she might still have thought it had she not seen at once that the idea was ludicrous.

Reluctant to continue thinking of him, she went to the classroom where she had left a pile of exercise books that needed correcting. Carrying them back to her bedroom, she set to work.

The long afternoon passed slowly, then dusk fell quickly, the way it always does in the East. She washed and made herself tidy before going down to supper, a light meal during the weekend and one she usually took with a couple of the other teachers who lived at the school. But tonight there was only herself and Madame Nadar in the dining room, though the bottle of wine on the table made Fleur wonder what was being celebrated, for Madame was frugal and not given to such extravagance.

But when the Principal finally disclosed the reason for the wine, the word "celebration" was not one that came to Fleur's mind. It was impossible for her to go with Nizea to the Khans' home in the mountains. Madame had no right to suggest it nor to look so disgruntled when she immediately said no. She had come here to work at the school, not to act as chaperone for one particular pupil, and especially not in that pupil's home. It had been difficult enough to visit Nizea each day in Teheran, but to go to the mountains and stay there for a period of weeks would allow her no freedom whatever. Worse still, she would suffocate in the rigid atmosphere that Mr. Khan imposed on his womenfolk.

Yet no matter what excuses she gave, she knew she had not allowed the real one to surface to her conscious mind. But surface it must. If she went on refusing to acknowledge the danger, she would be unable to marshal her defences. And defence was imperative. Only by maintaining her guard against the insidious attraction that was making her painfully aware of a man who, logic told her, could never make her anything but desperately unhappy, would she stand a chance of retaining her heart. There could never be anything between herself and Karim Khan. He was attracted to her—she knew that—had known it since the night he had driven her home from his father's house. But he would only want to flirt with her; to take sensuous pleasure in her fair coloring which was so different from that of his own countrywomen. Anything deeper and more lasting would be unthinkable for both of them.

"I hope you will reconsider it and change your mind," Madame Nadar was speaking again. "As you know I am under an obligation to Mr. Khan."

"It isn't *my* obligation, Madame." It was the first time

Fleur had stood her ground, and the Persian woman looked annoyed.

"I cannot force you to do as I ask, Miss Peters, nor would I try to break my contract with you. So you see I have no way in which I can make you change your mind other than to rely on your sense of responsibility."

"I fail to see what responsibility you are referring to, Madame."

"Do you not feel you have encouraged Nizea's ambition to write and given her cause to hope she might get her own way with her father?"

"I have encouraged all my pupils to stand up for what they believe in. I did no more for Nizea than for any of the other girls."

"But Nizea isn't like the other girls. She feels things more deeply—possibly because she *is* talented—and by encouraging her ideas you have created a rebel."

"A rebel because she wants to continue her education?" Fleur said bitterly. "If I had known her father was still living in the last century, I would . . ."

"There are many men who think the same way," Madame Nadar interrupted. "But to talk of it is futile." The plump hands fluttered. "Let us change the subject. As to the Khans' offer—you are free to do as you wish."

"I'll stay with Nizea for a couple of weeks," Fleur said hesitantly. She knew she was foolish to capitulate but after hasty reflection could not see any other way out. "But I'd like you to make it clear that I won't stay the entire summer."

"I'm sure Mr. Khan wouldn't expect it of you."

"Was it Mr. Karim Khan who made the suggestion?"

"Yes. But obviously with the family's approval."

Fleur's heart thumped heavily. So she had been right in thinking Karim Khan was attracted to her? Her sense of triumph quickly gave way to trepidation.

"Please make it clear to Mr. Khan that I must feel free to leave whenever I wish," she reiterated.

"I assure you there'll be no problems about that. And thank you for changing your mind. You won't regret it."

Fleur wished she could agree, but her intuition told her Madame was very wrong indeed.

Six

FLEUR rolled off the floating lilo and dipped her toes into the swimming pool. It was in a free form style with mosaic sides, and the water was heavily scented with jasmine. This was luxury indeed.

Keeping her eyes closed she tilted her face to the sun, enjoying the warmth of the rays and knowing she dare not bask for long lest they burn her delicate skin. She wriggled happily. It was so easy to grow used to idleness that it was hard to believe she had been here only a couple of weeks.

Luckily, the fears that had made her hesitate to accept the offer had not materialized, for Karim Khan had made no attempt to seek her out during either of the two weekends he had spent here since her arrival. Though piqued by his behavior, she was sensible enough to be glad of it.

He had obviously realized nothing could result from their friendship and had wisely decided not to pursue it.

But though logic told her to be glad, emotion made her feel otherwise, and when the son of the house was in residence she could not quiet the racing of her heart nor prevent self-consciousness from pervading every part of her body. It was almost as if his eyes were constantly upon her. She could even imagine him watching her now, though she knew him to be in Teheran, and was irritated that she could not be as indifferent to him as he now seemed to be toward her.

She lowered her head, and her hair fell forward over her face. She wore it loose during the day and it lay upon her shoulders like red-gold foam. Her skin was tanned to the color of honey; not the deep tan of Karim Khan, but a lighter shade that showed up the golden blonde flecks of hair on her forearms. Her apple-green bikini had brought forth squeals of delight from Nizea and had almost decided Fleur to wear a darker one-piece suit in its place— something she had every intention of doing if either of the Khan men elected to come and sun themselves by the pool. But during her time here neither of them had done so, and she had met them only briefly each Saturday evening when she and Nizea dined with Mrs. Khan and several of the other women from the household in the main salon where coffee and drinks were served: fruit drinks for those whose religion did not allow them to take alcohol and stronger drinks for the others.

Even here the younger Khan had made no attempt to say more to her than a brief greeting and had spent most of his time with the guests who were staying with them. Some came by car and some in the Khans' private helicopter. So far Fleur was the only European and had consequently felt very alien, though everyone always went out of the way to make her feel at home; she had found the women, in particular, to be extremely friendly. But she had always been glad to have Nizea as her excuse for not joining them in their private rooms later in the evening. Instead she would sit with her pupil and read or talk, using the time to try to make the girl accept the fact that she could not go against the plans her father had made for her.

She was not sure how well she was succeeding in this, and she thought of it now as she slipped into the water. It lapped against her skin like velvet and she leisurely swam a length and then floated on her back, reveling in the scent of jasmine and enjoying the warm rays of the sun above her and the cooling, buoyant water beneath. If only her friends in England could see her now. The thought made her smile, though it disappeared as she remembered Rory's annoyance when she had told him she was coming here.

"I never saw you as nursemaid to the Khans' daughter," he had protested. "You should have told Madame Nadar to pay her own debt of gratitude."

He would have been even angrier had he known that his reluctance to let her go away had confirmed her belief that she was doing the right thing in leaving Teheran. This at least might encourage him to go out with some of the other British and American girls living in the capital.

He had telephoned twice since she had arrived here, asking when she was coming back, but she had been evasive in her replies though she had already made up her mind she would not stay here longer than a month. But as two weeks had already passed without the son of the house making any attempt to occupy her time, she was not sure it was necessary for her to leave as early as she had intended. Staying here during the hot summer months would be infinitely preferable to life in the city.

She reached the side of the pool and climbed out, shaking her hair free of water. In five minutes the sun would dry it and it would once more be silky around her shoulders. She sank on to her mattress and reached for some suntan oil. She had forgotten to bring it with her and, deciding she might as well go in search of Nizea, she slipped on a white toweling robe, pulled the belt tightly around her waist and went through the luxuriant gardens towards the house.

As always the sight of its smooth white façade, the minaret-shaped roof, and the slender white pillars supporting the arched, covered terraces that ran along three sides brought a catch to her throat. The more she saw it, the more she appreciated its delicate yet oriental splendor. Amidst the heavy, variegated green foliage and profusion of flowers, it stood out like a gleaming pearl.

The seeming bareness of the interior had at first come as a shock to her eye. But now she was accustomed to it and saw that it allowed one to appreciate the shape and beautiful design of each room. The entrance hall was circular, with a graceful staircase curving upward like the stamen of a flower. The dining room was a long rectangle and the main salon a perfect oval; both with long narrow windows covered by shimmering white silk that diffused the brilliant white light. The floors were of marble: pale green onyx in the hall and shining white and gold in the main rooms and terraces. The ceilings were vaulted and blue as the summer sky after rain, while everywhere there were magnificent Persian rugs—glowing like jewels—either on the floor or hanging on the wall. Furniture was kept to a minimum though there was an abundance of velvet and satin cushions and small, ivory-inlaid tables laden with silver bowls of fruit and sweetmeats. Only the dining room was furnished in European style, with a long table and chairs of smoky blue glass and steel.

Quickly Fleur ran up to Nizea's room, where the girl was resting on her bed.

"Do you believe one can write only from experience?" Nizea asked the moment Fleur came in.

"It depends. Why do you ask?"

"I was thinking of Françoise Sagan. She wrote a wonderful book when she was only seventeen."

"Are you going to prove it can be done a second time?"

"I wish I could." There was a heavy sigh. "The trouble is I don't have a plot."

"Why not write about your childhood? From what you've told me, it sounds fascinating."

"It was dull."

"Not the way you describe it. All those lovely incidents with your Aunt Maideh. The intrigues and arguments, and how the women manage to get their own way with the men. Didn't you ever keep a diary?"

"I've got ten. I started keeping them when I was seven." She reached under the bedclothes and pulled out a leatherbound notebook. "It's strange you should tell me to write about my childhood. I was reading one of my diaries just before you came in. Read it, and tell me what you think."

Fleur took the notebook and perched on the edge of a chair, her shapely legs stretching in front of her. Nizea wrote in a scrawl, but soon the power of what she had written superceded the difficulty of deciphering it, and Fleur was held enthralled. Here was the outpouring of a charming girl, pausing on the brink of womanhood to look back on her childhood. With warm humor she evoked her life in a cloistered environment, where she had learned to temper her curiosity with discretion; learned, too, that it was better to flatter in order to get what she wanted than to indulge in tantrums.

At the end of a dozen pages Fleur closed the diary with a deep sigh. "If I ever had any regrets in coming to Iran, then being able to say you were once my pupil will make it all worthwhile."

"Will it really, Miss Peters?"

"Really," Fleur smiled, and then said what she had been meaning to say for several days. "Don't you think you might call me Fleur? Each time you say Miss Peters I feel like an old spinster."

"How old are you?"

"Twenty-five—definitely a spinster by Persian standards." She stood up. "Though I don't think I'll live to be a very old maid unless I change out of this wet costume. But I just wanted to pop in and see if you were all right."

"Are you going down to the pool again?"

"Yes, but not to swim. We can sit in the shade and do some work."

"I'm on holiday," Nizea pouted.

"Life is one long holiday for you," Fleur teased and went to her own room to change into a sun dress.

She was glad she had replenished her wardrobe extrav-

agantly before coming to Iran, though the clothes that
had pleased her so much when she had bought them in
England looked ordinary compared with the beautiful out-
fits worn by the Persian women who came to visit the
Khans. Their jewelry too astounded her, making her realize the immense wealth that existed in the country: a
wealth that made the Greek shipping tycoons seem poor
by comparison. The Middle East was the world of the future, she thought soberly as she buttoned the bodice of
her white cotton sun suit. She only hoped that the power
that money brought would not corrupt them.

For the next couple of hours Fleur and Nizea sat in the
garden where the riotously blooming flowers would have
made the covers of any seed packet look insipid. It was as
if technicolor had gone mad and, even with dark glasses,
the blazing scarlet, chrome yellows, and vivid greens were
blinding to the eye.

Petunias and pansies seemed to be the rage, though the
ubiquitous rose flourished everywhere. There was a bush
of two-colored roses that Fleur found unfailingly astonishing, and she looked at it regularly each day. The outer petals were yellow and, as each new bud unfolded into a full
blown rose, the inner petals were seen to be scalloped.
Fountains tinkled everywhere, and narrow canals filled
with floating red petals crisscrossed lawns that were kept
green by the continuous labor of servants. There was a
quality about the atmosphere of the garden that made it
easy for Fleur to imagine Karim Khan's ancestors sitting
here holding court; a lordly, black-bearded Khan in
jewel-studded robes, lying on a couch surrounded by the
women of his harem.

So clear was this vision that she ceased talking to Nizea

and watched as a servant approached with iced tea. As she sipped the fragrant brew she asked Nizea how far her family could trace back their line.

"Hundreds of years," the girl said proudly. "It is said that the true Persian originally came from Southern Russia and settled on the high plains of Iran. Some of them went on to India so I suppose I could have ended up in Delhi wearing a sari!"

"You've given me a very generalized account of your ancestors," Fleur said drily. "Can't you be more specific with the details?"

The younger girl burst out laughing. "If you really want to know about my great-great-greats, you'd better talk to my father. He knows every branch and twig of the family tree! For myself, I couldn't care less."

"You've no poetry in your soul," Fleur teased and leaned forward to take a sweetmeat. Then she stopped. Unless she exercised some control over the habit of nibbling these delicious confections, she would have to start letting out the seams of her dresses.

"Karim's just as proud of his ancestors as my father is," Nizea commented. "We once had some English guests who asked him if he thought of himself as an Arab, and I thought he'd have a fit!"

It was a question that Fleur knew evoked a strong, negative response in most Persians, since the Arabs had once been their conquerors.

"In fact, if you talk to Karim about our family," Nizea went on, "he'll make it even more interesting than my father will."

Fleur was sure of this and equally sure that the last thing in the world she wanted was to talk to Karim Khan about anything. The less she saw of him the better for her peace of mind.

There was the drone of an aircraft in the sky but the trees prevented them from seeing it. The sound came nearer, and then by the rough beat of engines they knew it was a helicopter.

"That's Papa and Karim," Nizea announced.

"So early?" Fleur questioned.

"It's Thursday, don't forget, and sometimes Papa stops at lunchtime."

Fleur smiled. "I still can't get used to having a weekend begin on Thursday night."

"That's because you keep Sunday, too."

"Only from habit. It's not because I'm religious."

"I'm not religious either," Nizea stated. "How can I accept a religion that regards women as the chattels of men? Don't you think it's dreadful?"

Fleur refused to answer. She had learned long ago that Nizea was indiscreet and quite likely to repeat any opinions discussed here on a less private occasion.

"Persian women are far less downtrodden today than they were ten years ago," she said diplomatically.

"*I'm* not."

"Your life is extremely emancipated compared with your grandmother's," Fleur insisted. "You should look on the positive side of things, not the negative."

"Now you're speaking like a teacher."

"I *am* a teacher."

"I don't think of you as one." Nizea edged forward in her chair, careful not to move her left leg. "You're far too beautiful to be a teacher, Fleur. You should be a film star or a model. Some job where you can use your looks."

"I prefer to use my mind. I'll have that far longer than I'll have my looks."

Nizea frowned. "It's hard to argue with you. You're too logical."

"Did I hear someone say that a woman is logical?" a melodious voice asked in amusement.

Both girls swung round as the heavy green leaves parted, and Karim Khan's tall, lithe figure emerged. As always he was well dressed but, because of the heat, his suit was of the lightest silk.

"What woman is logical?" he repeated.

"Fleur is," said his sister.

The man turned and allowed his eyes to move over the golden-limbed body of the tall, slender girl lounging on the basket chair in front of him.

Fleur knew she made a striking picture with her red-gold hair vivid against the green background of leaves. Even so she was unprepared for the long and appraising stare to which she was being subjected, and her body grew warm. Resisting the urge to set her feet on the ground and run away, she lowered her lashes and tried to look unconcerned.

"The rest here has done you good, Miss Peters," Karim Khan said. "You look like your old self again."

"My old self?" She lifted her head but made sure their eyes did not meet.

"The way you looked the first day you came to my father's house."

She noticed he did not say "our house," the way an Englishman would have referred to the home he shared with his parents. But then the Persians, though they had a strong sense of family, also had a strong sense of property and, as long as Ibrahim Khan was alive, the family house would be referred to as his.

"I'm beginning to think I've been idle too long," she murmured. "I must think of returning to Teheran."

"In this heat you are better off here." The voice was liquid soft, but the eyes were narrow slits.

"You can't talk about going back so soon," Nizea interpolated. "You promised you'd stay at least a month."

"I'm not going back this week," Fleur said hastily. "I was merely telling your . . . telling Mr. Khan that I was thinking about it."

"What Miss Peters means," the man said, looking first at his sister and then returning his gaze to Fleur, "is that she wants me to know she is keeping her options open."

"I don't understand what that means," Nizea said and was prevented from having her curiosity satisfied by the arrival of a manservant and a nurse, who carefully placed her in her wheelchair for the return trip to her room.

"I'll be in to have dinner with you at the usual time," Fleur said and half rose to leave the garden with her pupil.

But her way was barred by Karim Khan and, not sure if he wished to talk to her about his sister, she resumed her seat. They were both silent until the wheelchair turned a bend in the path and was out of sight. Then the man spoke.

"Why are you always in such a hurry to run away from me?"

Fleur was tempted to say, "Because I'm afraid of you," and though one part of her was curious to know how he would have replied to such a statement, common sense told her it would be a foolish thing to admit. He would see it as flirtatiousness and, since he was obviously attracted to her, she must avoid doing anything to arouse him further.

"You haven't answered my question," he said. His eyes were fixed on her, his body so close to her chair that, short of pushing him away, she could not rise and leave.

"I find you . . . you make me nervous," she murmured.

"Why?" His eyes narrowed further. "It can't be anything I've done, so it must be something I've said. Is it because I don't agree with you about my sister?"

She seized on this as being a reasonable excuse for her to avoid him. "Yes, Mr. Kahn, it is."

"But there's more to it than that, I think," he continued. "It isn't only my attitude toward Nizea that you dislike. There's something else about me that worries you; that puts you on the defensive—like a frightened doe."

"A frightened doe." The words had a poetic ring and were also a remarkably apt way of describing how she felt. More than ever he seemed to represent strength and authority, and her fear of him deepened. She stared at him, not seeing a man of the twentieth century but an image of an earlier Khan. The pale suit turned into a rich satin one, lavishly jeweled. The thick black hair that grew low on his nape suddenly grew even lower, though most of it was hidden by a heavily swathed turban. The finely cut mouth was hidden too—by a heavy black beard that gave fierceness to his face. Her breath caught in her throat, and she put up her hand, feeling her heart beating fast beneath her fingertips.

"What is it?" Karim Khan said and caught her arm. "Why are you looking at me so strangely?"

"I'm sorry." She gave a shake of her head. The picture of the past and present fused into one and the Mogul became the man. "For a moment I saw you as if . . . as if you were one of your ancestors."

His mouth parted to show gleaming white teeth, though the movement could never have been called a smile. "From your expression I doubt whether it was a pleasant picture. How did you see me, Miss Peters—as a masochistic conqueror looking for infidels or as a tyrant beating one of my many wives?"

"Neither," she said coldly, hiding her amazement at the quickness of his mind. "But I admit I . . . I put you into something more colorful than the suit you're wearing."

He looked down at his jacket and at the same time released his grip on her arm. "I will be glad to change into something less formal," he said. "Perhaps you will join me for a swim?"

"I couldn't."

"Couldn't or won't?"

" 'Shouldn't' is probably the better word," she explained. "I don't think it would be right for me to swim with you. I'm here as Nizea's teacher."

"You are here as her friend," he said softly. "And if I were not afraid of scaring you even more than you are already, I would tell you that you were here because I want you to be."

Fleur looked at the ground and determinedly took his words at their face value.

"I'm glad you take an interest in your sister's welfare, Mr. Kahn. I'm trying to be a companion to her, but I still don't think it right for me to go swimming with you. Customs here are different from those in England."

"You are behind the times. When we entertain European visitors, we follow European customs."

"But you aren't entertaining a European, Mr. Khan. I'm not here as your guest."

He moved back a step, as if irritated, and this gave her the opportunity of jumping to her feet. She still had to tilt her head to look at him, because he was so tall, but she felt at less disadvantage now that she was standing.

"Please don't treat me as a guest, Mr. Khan. If you do, you will embarrass me and make it difficult for me to remain here."

Slowly he surveyed her, his eyes crinkling at the corners as if he were amused. "All this because I asked you to have a swim with me! I had no idea that treating you as a guest was a sign of disrespect."

"You know very well it isn't." Crossly she faced him.

"Then why such strict adherence to protocol?"

"Because your father expects it of me."

The amusement left Karim Khan's face, and Fleur wished she had thought to mention his father earlier. Obviously this was the best way of bringing the younger man back to a recognition of his responsibilities; to remind him that this did not include flirting with European women.

"I regret I will not have the pleasure of swimming with you," he murmured, "but at least I've had the pleasure of seeing you in a swimsuit."

"You haven't," she said, startled. "I never swim when you're here."

"I'm well aware of that." His tone was ironic. "But I saw you once when you did not know I was nearby. You wore a green bikini—and you swam like a fish." His right hand gestured towards her hair. "With such a crowning glory perhaps I should say—goldfish!"

"To know you were watching me through the bushes," she said with some austerity, "makes me *feel* like a goldfish. All I lack is the bowl!"

He gave the same uninhibited laugh she had heard from him once before. It was at variance with the precise way he spoke and dressed, and she had the feeling there were many aspects of him that people did not know. It might even be more apt to say, had not been *allowed* to know.

"If you will excuse me, Mr. Khan, I'd like to go to my room and rest."

"You can rest here and talk to me."

"I thought you wanted to change into something cooler."

"I have already been sufficiently chilled by your manner!" Involuntarily she smiled, and he was quick to see it. "You have a dimple in your cheek," he said softly, "and it adds—if such a thing were possible—to your beauty."

"Please don't say that," she said quickly.

"Why not? It's true."

"You mustn't talk to me like this."

"Are you always embarrassed when a man pays you compliments?"

"If he's my employer."

"I'm not your employer."

"You are his son; and in this country a father and son speak the same language."

For a few seconds he surveyed her, his arms folded across his chest. "That is true, Miss Pteers. Here, a father and son try to speak with one voice, a fact that regrettably does not apply in many other parts of the world. In the West, for example, the young like to hold the opposite view from their parents—though they usually revert to it as they mature."

"I wasn't being critical of what happens here," she said hurriedly. "I was merely stating a fact."

"So was I. But I don't know many facts about *you*, Miss Peters. Were you emancipated when you were a student, or did you always follow the carefully thought out path you are following now?"

"My parents always encouraged me to think for myself," she said stiffly.

"They didn't mind you coming to Iran?"

"Why should they have? It's only for a year and at the end of that time I'll be returning home."

"To marry an Englishman?"

"If I fall in love with one."

"Would you allow yourself to fall in love with a man who wasn't?"

"It isn't a question of allowing." Her words were chosen with care. "You make it sound as if one can decide with whom one falls in love."

"One can." He spoke with a sharpness that surprised her. "One can, Miss Peters. I assure you of that."

Abruptly he turned on his heel and walked away. He had never before left her without making some polite excuse, and she knew that something had annoyed him.

The knowledge gave her an empty feeling deep inside. So he thought that one could choose whom one loved. Well, maybe a man like Karim Khan could, but she couldn't. To her, love would come whether she wanted it or not; overcoming her inhibitions and overwhelming her good sense. She would love first and, not until later, would she question whether or not she was right. It was odd that she should know this—almost as if she had already fallen in love and knew it would not come to fruition. Yet she was not in love. There was no man to whom she had given her heart, or even a tiny portion of it.

Gathering up her books, she hurried away. It was too early to change, but at least in her bedroom she would be safe from intrusion.

Seven

AS *Fleur was changing, a servant* brought her a message from Mrs. Khan asking her to join the family for dinner at eight o'clock.

Fleur's instant reaction was that Karim Khan had suggested it, and her first impulse was to say no. Unfortunately, she could not think of a reasonable excuse and, reluctant to give a feeble one, she had no option but to accept. But she would make it clear to the lordly son of the house that he could not command her as easily as he commanded other women. She was sure he did command them—it was apparent in the way he looked and spoke to her—as if he knew the effect he had on the female sex. One look from those smouldering dark eyes of his, and a woman could easily be persuaded to lose her head. And all in the name of love when it was nothing more than sex.

Her lips curled scornfully. Sex. Nature's cunning way

of making sure the human race continued. Fleur knew she
was deliberately being cynical, using it as a defence
against the emotional response this handsome man
aroused in her. Yet all she was doing was making herself
aware how strong one's instincts are and how hard it is to
fight them. The attraction she and Karim Khan felt for
each other came from their dissimilarities: from his desire
to conquer and from hers to resist; from his determination
to take and her refusal to give. More important still, she
feared him and, because he saw her fear as the first sign
of weakening, he was becoming all the more determined
in his pursuit. But how could she openly warn him he was
wasting his time when he had not made any definite move
towards her and all she had to go on was her intuition?

So intent was she on this problem that she finished
dressing automatically. It was a good thing, for had she
given it any thought she would have been dissatisfied with
everything in her wardrobe. But the knowledge that her
simple clothes could never compete with the luxurious
ones of the rich Persian women had at least prevented her
from making the attempt, and she was amused to see she
had instinctively chosen the simplest of her evening
dresses: a white silk with a round neckline that only
hinted at the soft curves of her breasts. A narrow gold
cord encircled her waist and gold sandals glinted on her
slender feet as her long skirts swayed around them.

The sun had lightened her hair and tonight it was more
gold than red. It fell in loose waves from a center part. It
was a naïve style that she hoped would warn Karim she
was not the sophisticated Englishwoman he wanted her to
be but a young schoolteacher who had led a cloistered

life—despite the fact that she came from a country which, he considered, allowed its women complete freedom.

On her way to the salon she went to see Nizea who, though dismayed at being left to have dinner with her old nanny, was delighted that Fleur was dining with her family.

"Mama said they were having some interesting guests tonight," she said. "If you get finished early enough, come in and tell me how the evening went."

Promising she would, if it were not too late, Fleur went down to the hall. The sound of voices and the clink of glasses came from the main salon, but she hesitated to enter it, embarrassed to go forward on her own.

She was still standing by the stairs when Ibrahim Khan appeared through the doorway on her left. He wore a dinner jacket of the same excellent cut as his son's, and the resemblance between the two men struck her strongly. Add thirty years to the younger man—plus a beard—and he would be a replica of his father.

"I'm delighted you were able to join us for dinner," her host said. "Are you nervous about entering the room on your own?"

"A little."

He proffered his arm and, taken aback by the gesture, she put her hand on it.

Their entrance caused a momentary silence in the salon, then he led her towards his wife who looked every inch the matriarch of the house in a brocade gown that was almost stiff enough to stand on its own. A double row of large diamonds sparkled around her throat, and a waterfall of diamonds cascaded from each ear.

"Lovely to see you." The woman smiled at Fleur as if

she were a cherished guest and not her daughter's companion. "I have a little surprise for you."

With a gasp of pleasure Fleur recognized the man standing beside Madame Khan as her godfather and erstwhile tutor from her university days, whom she had last seen a month before leaving England.

"Uncle Desmond! What on earth are you doing here? And why didn't you let me know you were coming?"

"It was all arranged at a few days' notice." He drew her forward to kiss her.

He looked exactly as she remembered him: untidy in an ill-fitting dinner jacket with a straggle of gray hair on the dome of his head and a long, lugubrious face. But the blue eyes were full of humor, and the lines around them were wise ones.

"Why didn't you let me know you were coming?" she asked, still delighted by the surprise of seeing him when she had thought him safely ensconced in the cloistered quietness of the groves of Academe.

"I only knew of my trip a week ago. Your father gave me your address at the school and . . ."

"But I wrote and told them I was staying with one of my pupils," she intervened.

"They weren't sure if you were still here. Your letter wasn't explicit on that point. Anyway, when Madame Nadar said where you were, I immediately rang up Mr. Khan," he smiled at his host, "whom I have known for many years and who had already extended an invitation to me to join him here."

"Which he had thought he would be too busy to accept until he knew *you* were staying with us," Ibrahim Khan said with dry humor.

"The excuse was genuine, my friend," Desmond Anderson said. "But once I knew Fleur was here, I rearranged my schedule. I dared not come all the way to Iran and not see my goddaughter."

"Then I will leave you alone with her to satisfy yourself that we are not treating her harshly," his host smiled, leaving his two English guests to talk together.

Fleur looked at her godfather fondly, surprised how pleased she was to see someone from England. It made her parents seem closer and also made her feel less of an alien.

"Being a foreigner in someone else's country makes you feel terribly alone," she said. "You start to question your own attitudes—as if you can no longer take for granted all the things you've accepted and valued—and you start having doubts about everything."

"That's why there's some value in having an English club where you can go," Desmond Anderson replied. "Why haven't you been to the Embassy? I'm sure the Ambassador would make you welcome. He and your father were at school together."

"I don't want to get in with the diplomatic set," Fleur replied. "I didn't have anything in common with them in England, and I'd like them even less out here. They lead such insular lives."

"I thought you were homesick for a bit of the British way of life!"

"I am. But . . ."

"There's always a 'but' in everything," her godfather said.

"Not enough of one to make me want to return home."

The gray eyebrows were raised. "Never?"

"Oh, no." She flushed. "I didn't mean that. But I'll be quite happy to remain here until my contract is ended."

"How do you like the Khans?"

"They've been charming to me."

"Does that include Karim?"

"They're all charming." Her voice was even but the glass of mineral water she was holding shook in her hand. Quickly she pretended to drink some. "I've got so used to drinking this stuff that I'll hate water when I get back to England!"

"You may not get back to England at all if you don't drink it," her godfather smiled.

They were still discussing drinks and food when Karim Khan disengaged himself from a group of people and came to join them. His skin seemed even more golden by comparison with the startling white of his silk shirt. He was not as tall as Desmond Anderson, who was nearly six feet four, but his shoulders were broader and his carriage extremely erect.

"I didn't realize you knew Miss Peters," he said. "My father didn't mention it to me."

"I've known Fleur since she was a twinkle in her father's eye."

"And now she brings a glitter to the eyes of other men," the young man concluded.

"You are never short of a compliment, Mr. Khan," Fleur said. "Are all your countrymen as adept as you?"

"I must deny that I was paying you a compliment," he smiled. "All I did was to state a *fact*."

"Does that mean *compliments* are usually lies?"

His lips curved and, as always, she was fascinated by

the lower one. "I must be on my guard when I speak with you."

Desmond Anderson moved beside her, and she saw that Ibrahim Khan was leading their guests in to dinner. Glad of a chance to end a conversation that could have become more serious than she wanted, she accompanied her godfather to the dining room.

The table could seat forty, and as many silver place settings were laid out on its surface. Individual silver and gold bowls held rose water for washing one's fingers, and a silver ring held a silk damask napkin. The food, when it came, was sumptuous, with huge mounds of caviar set in ice and served in silver bowls. This was followed by numerous pilafs: lentils and beans, rice with various kinds of meat, lima beans and lamb, and chicken and apricot. Finally there was a variety of desserts accompanied by the inevitable yoghurt and a magnificent array of fresh fruit, some of which had obviously been flown in from abroad.

Fleur tried to do justice to the dinner but found it impossible, for every time she looked up from her plate she saw Karim Khan watching her from the other side of the table. She had been delighted to find she was not sitting next to him but, after the first course had been served, would gladly have had him beside her. At least then she could have avoided his penetrating gaze. As it was, whenever she lifted her head it was to see him focusing upon her. She knew her godfather had noticed it and was glad Ibrahim Khan was seated at the far end of the table; otherwise he would have become aware of it, too.

"Karim seems rather taken with you," Desmond Anderson murmured as they rose to leave the dining room.

"It's not because I've given him any encouragement.

I'm very careful to keep my place while I'm living here," Fleur said.

"Wise girl. These ancient Persian families have a strong sense of tradition. For a Westerner to try and become part of it is courting trouble."

They crossed the hall and, at the salon door she stopped, knowing that the women would go to Madame Khan's quarters, where they would remain until their menfolk were ready to take their leave.

"I'm surprised Ibrahim Khan still sticks to this old custom," Desmond Anderson commented.

"I'm not," Fleur replied and hastily moved to the stairs as she saw Karim Khan approaching. "I doubt if I'll see you again tonight, Uncle Desmond. What time are you leaving tomorrow?"

"After lunch. We'll have plenty of time to talk in the morning."

"Why don't you come down again later, Miss Peters?" Karim Khan's voice was vibrant in her ear. "The women won't be retiring for long."

"I'm feeling tired," she lied and slipped past him to the stairs.

Only when she was alone in her room did she chide herself for letting her nerves get the better of her. The evening was still young and she was not in the least tired. On the contrary, excitement had keyed her up, and she knew it would be hours before she could sleep.

She went to see Nizea and found the girl engaged in a complicated game of backgammon with her elderly companion.

"It'll soon be over," Nizea proclaimed. "Then we can talk."

"Not tonight," Fleur said hastily. "I'd just as soon go to bed."

Before the girl could argue, Fleur closed the door and returned to her own room where she settled in a chair on the balcony. Below her the garden was illumined here and there by little pools of light. The night was silent except for the faint sound of waterfalls and the occasional call of a bird. She tried to read but felt a restless longing to go down and walk along the narrow twisting paths; to dabble her hands in the pool where the goldfish swam; and to touch gently the petals of the lilies that lay, in waxlike perfection, in their watery graves.

Unbidden, she remembered Karim Khan calling her a goldfish and was glad she had not known he was watching her. From now on she would not swim without making sure he was miles away. How had he had the opportunity of seeing her without her knowing? The book slipped between her fingers and fell unheeded to the ground, and she sat for a long time thinking of him and trying to guess what future he would have and with whom he would share it. It was odd that he was still single; as an only son it was incumbent on him to produce an heir, and she was surprised that this duty had not urged him into marriage.

The night air sharpened, and a sickle moon gave sparkle to the stars that lay cool in their background of black velvet. The watch on her wrist showed midnight, and she rose and went into her bedroom. The room seemed to stifle her, and again she felt the urge to walk in the fresh air. She went into the corridor and tiptoed to the head of the stairs. There were no sounds from below and she surmised that everyone had retired for the night. Quietly she went down to the marble hall, careful not to let her high heels make any sound. The long terrace was deserted, the tall slender columns that supported it resembling pale, unlit candles. For a moment she stood there with the moonlight drenching her white gown. With a brief backward glance she stepped forward, lifted her skirts slightly, and sped along the path in the direction of the rose garden.

Roses grew everywhere in abundance, but in one particular area huge clusters of the flowers formed arbors whose perfume made the air shiver with its intensity. Walking here was like drifting in a rose petal sea. Even in the dark night air the scent was overpowering as she wandered from one bush to another, pausing occasionally to look at a perfect bloom.

From somewhere close by, a waterfall tinkled as it splashed into a marble basin. She hadn't remembered seeing one here, and she wandered along a twisting path in search of it. Yes, there it was, straight ahead of her: a pale urn, graceful as a Grecian vase, with crystal clear water spouting from two sides. She trailed her hand in the basin, then touched her water-cooled fingers to her cheek.

"In the moonlight your hair shines like silver," a deep voice said and with an audible gasp she swung round and saw Karim Khan.

"Are you spying on me again?" she accused.

"I followed you into the garden. Do you call that spying?"

"Why did you follow me?"

"Don't you know?"

All she knew was that she should not have asked the question, and she took a step backward. He did not stop her, and she took another step away from him, then swiftly went into the rose garden again, intent on returning to the house. As she ran, her skirt flared out around her and a silky layer of the material caught against one of the bushes. She stopped in midflight and turned to disentangle herself from the thorns, seeing Karim Khan's dark figure almost behind her as she did so.

This time her voice shook with anger. "Will you please leave me alone? Why do you persist in following he?"

"I'm bowing to Fate," he said heavily and then leaned forward and expertly removed the thorns that were binding her to the bush. Her skirt fell around her ankles again, and he stepped to one side. "You are free to go," he said, "but I hope you won't."

As he had helped to rescue her and had probably got several thorns in his flesh in the process, it seemed ungracious to run away immediately.

"I was delighted to see Desmond Anderson," she said as composedly as she could. "He was not only my tutor at the university but a great friend of my family."

"Is that what makes him acceptable?" Karim Khan's voice was heavy. "Does a man have to be a great friend of your family before you will smile at him?"

"Of course not."

"Then what do I have to do to make you smile at *me?*"

"You . . . you don't have to do anything. I . . . I often smile at you."

"Without looking at me," he said savagely. "Sometimes you remind me of a cat . . . they don't like staring you in the eyes, either."

"Nor do dogs," she said quickly. "Most animals refuse to look at you for more than a few seconds at a time."

"But you aren't an animal," he muttered, "you are a

woman. A beautiful, desirable woman with eyes like green peridots, and I'm crazy about you."

He didn't reach out for her so much as enfold her within his arms, wrapping them around her as if they were a barrier of protection. It gave Fleur the most extraordinary feeling of coming home and, though she tried to resist, it was impossible. But if she could not resist, neither would she capitulate, and she remained tense as a quivering arrow within his hold.

"I'm crazy about you," he repeated. "From the moment I saw you I haven't been able to get you out of my mind, and now I can't get you out of my heart."

"Don't say that," she gasped.

"Why not? You don't know how I want to hold you like this. To touch you . . . to feel your body against mine. The warmth of your skin; the scent of your breath; the mystery of your mouth. *Darling . . .*"

He gave her no chance to draw away before his mouth fastened on hers. Its pressure was gentle but inexorable and, though she struggled, he did not release her but went on moving his lips over hers. At last she knew the touch of his mouth and realized that his skin was as soft as it looked; smooth as velvet except where one felt the hardness of his cheekbones and the firm line of his jaw. She put her hands against his chest to push him away, but he caught them and pulled them behind her, making it impossible for her to escape. She tried to turn her head to one side to escape his devouring mouth and as he felt her desperate movements, he raised his lips slightly above hers and spoke against them.

"You are too honest to say you don't want me to kiss you," he said. "You have wanted it as much as I have."

"That still doesn't make it right. Please let me go."

"I can't."

"Of course, you can," she said angrily.

"No, Fleur, I can't." He moved his hand along the slender column of her neck until his long, brown fingers rested against the whiteness of her throat.

"Do you think I wouldn't let you go if I could?" he demanded. "Don't you know how hard I've fought against my feelings for you? I've tried with all my strength to put you out of my heart, but it's useless. I want you," he whispered. "I'll have no peace until you're mine."

"You're crazy to talk like that."

"Maybe I am. But it's a craziness I can't fight any longer."

Looking up into his face her fear grew. If moonlight had robbed her hair of color, it had also done the same for him. But instead of making him pale, it made him dark, giving him a sinister quality that sent the blood rushing turbulently through her body. There was no doubt he wanted her. She felt it in the trembling of his limbs and the heavy throbbing of the thighs that were pressing against hers. But to want did not mean the right to take, and he had to be made to see this.

With a mounting sense of danger Fleur knew why she had always been so much on her guard with this startlingly handsome man whose features had etched themselves upon her brain. She loved him—blindly, willfully, and against all logic she loved this demanding, dominating stranger. And he *was* a stranger. Strange in his looks, his traditions, his culture, and in the way he intended to live his life. The thought of the future was the most frightening of all, and she knew that unless she fought against her love for him, she would be irrevocably lost.

"You don't love me," she said tremulously. "You want me because I'm different from the women you've known. I've answered you back—made you angry and aware of me."

"If it were only that," he groaned, "do you think I would have succumbed like this? You aren't the first woman with a serpent's tongue."

"Perhaps I'm the first *English* woman who hasn't fallen for you!"

"I knew you'd say that." His smile was sharp and sudden. "But you're wrong there, too. Do you think it's your lily-white skin that attracts me? That I desire you because you're different from the other women I have known?"

His fingers moved from her throat, hovered above her breast and then lowered to encircle her waist. He drew her hard against his chest, and she felt his heart pounding fiercely.

"What's so unique about one pale-faced Western woman that I should want her above all others?" he went on remorselessly. "Would it surprise you to know that I've had more than I can count?"

"I'm not interested in your past!" she cried. "Nor do I care about your future."

"But you've got to care. I won't have you thinking that I want you only because you're different."

"It can't be anything else," she panted, trying to twist away from him. "You don't know me. We're strangers to each other—aliens."

"All men are aliens to all women," he said heavily. "Only their need for each other makes them compatible—the way you and I will be compatible once you have learned to accept me."

"I'll never accept you! Can't you understand that?"

For answer he caught back her hair and twisted it round his hand, then used the tautened strands to pull her face close to his. His features became a blur and all she could see were the black, dilated pupils of his eyes.

"I'll never let you go," he murmured and once more took possession of her mouth.

It was impossible to defend herself against the onslaught of his passion. It overcame her, dissolving her reason, and making her abandon her defence. The blood that coursed through her veins was like the water from the fountains of this Persian garden, rising higher and higher to the skillful play of his hands. Her lips parted and her head fell back against his shoulder. His tongue accepted her surrender and moved inside the warm sweetness of her mouth. Fleur's body awakened as though it had been given another life. Every limb trembled and her innermost parts pulsated with an urge to take and to be taken. It was a new emotion, and it thrilled her with dread. She would never be the same again. Desires had been released which, even if she denied them, could never be totally absorbed or totally forgotten. Yet she could not accept this man. To do so would be death to her freedom.

Desperately she pushed against him, pummeling her fists upon his chest. Her attempts to be free only excited him more, and his tongue penetrated deeper. She tried to claw at the side of his face and instead felt his hair beneath her fingers. It was thick and silky as cream, and she began to shake as though with fever. How could she push him away when she wanted him close, when she wanted to cradle his body against hers, to feel the weight of his head on her breast, the tautness of his stomach on the softness of her own? Like a leaf she shook against him and where her strength had failed to gain her her freedom, her weakness did it for her. With a murmur of distress he raised his face away from hers and swung her off the ground and into his arms.

"Don't be afraid of me," he said tenderly and moved with her to a marble bench. He placed her upon it and sat close beside her.

"Fleur," he whispered. "Fleur. I've wanted to call you by your name for so long yet I never dared. Do you find it strange to hear me say it?"

"No." With an enormous effort she made the word firm. "Calling people by their first name doesn't mean anything these days."

"Not in your world, my princess, but it does in mine. Fleur." He nuzzled his face into her hair, breathing it in deeply. "How aptly named you are. You're like a flower. A scarlet and gold rose with the petals still tightly closed and the heart of it hidden from everyone's sight but mine."

"Not yours, either," she said sharply and tried to rise.

His arms pulled her back down. "There are things we must talk about first. There is much I wish to say to you."

"I don't want to hear it!" she cried and was so near breaking point that her voice cracked.

Nothing could more easily have gained his sympathy, and he was instantly contrite. "Darling, don't be frightened. I'll never hurt you. But you've always attacked me with such spirit that I've thought you stronger than you are."

"I'm not at all strong," she said shakily and this time was able to rise unhindered.

"No one will ever take advantage of your weakness again," he said. "I will cherish you for the rest of my life."

"Then let me go free," she whispered and, picking up her skirts, ran out of the rose garden.

She did not cease running until the façade of the house came in sight, its marble gleaming almost iridescent in the moonlight. Only then did she slow her steps and let her skirt drop to the ground. The hem was bedraggled, and the bodice of her dress was crumpled from Karim's hold. She put the back of her hand to her lips. They felt bruised and swollen, but she knew it was only the tingling from the hardness of his mouth. There were steps behind her, and she swung round nervously, tensed for another onslaught from him. But this time the man watching her was older, the lower portion of his face masked by a black beard.

"You have been out in the garden, Miss Peters?" Ibrahim Khan asked.

"For a b-breath of fresh air," she stammered. "I'm j-just going to my room. Good-night, Mr. Khan." He nodded, and she knew his eyes remained on her as she turned and ran up the stairs. As she reached the top she heard his voice again, harder and more inflexible.

"So you have been in the garden, too, my son."

Not waiting to hear any more, Fleur rushed down the corridor to the haven of her room.

Eight

No *matter how many times Fleur told* herself that people of different cultures could live successfully side by side, she knew there were many instances where this did not apply.

The Persians were a case in point. Though they had been conquered by Arab invaders who had taken over their country in the sixth century, they still saw them as enemies and felt a greater affinity with Southern Russia and India.

More than any other race in this region of the world, the Persians took pleasure in their identity. They might send their children abroad to learn trades and professions, but they had no fear that their children would not wish to return. Indeed, even when separated by thousands of miles, families still maintained strong links with each other, marrying within the Faith and within their race.

Because she knew this, Fleur was convinced she could never have a future with Karim. He had said he wanted her, and the passion of his kisses had shown this to be true. But wanting did not imply loving and, even if it did, then loving would still not imply marriage.

Hour after hour she paced the floor, knowing she was faced with a problem from which she could not escape— except by running away.

If only she could take a love affair lightly, the way so many of her friends did. Yet though she had often tried to overcome this attitude, she had not been able to do so. To give herself to a man, she needed to be in love with him and, to her, love meant marriage. That she would fall in love with someone whose religion and culture made marriage impossible was something she had never envisaged. But it had happened and she must face the fact and decide what to do. But first, for a few dangerous moments, she would revel in the love she felt for this strange and wonderfully dynamic man. How she ached to feel his strength and tenderness, to arouse his desire, and then assuage it.

Fleetingly she wondered what sort of life she would have if she gave in to him. It would bring her a happiness she had never known before, but it would be of short duration. Passion did not last forever, and family commitments would inevitably exert their influence on him and turn him from her. What would happen to her then? Would she be able to accept a subsidiary role? To live with him in the shadows knowing he also lived in the sunlight with a wife and children? If she accepted Karim's love, there was no other way their future could evolve;

and since this was a future she was unable to accept, her decision was already made for her.

Fatigue placed dark fingers beneath her green eyes which no amount of skillful powdering could disguise next morning. To draw attention elsewhere, she wore mascara on her gold-tipped lashes and applied a deeper than usual coral lipstick on a mouth still slightly swollen from the hungry ardor of Karim's kisses. She was still shattered by the events of last night and knew it was going to take time to pull herself together. For the moment she must rely on her will power to get her through the day; and she thanked heaven that Karim would be going back to Teheran with Desmond. At least it would cut the weekend short, and before the next one came around she would make arrangements to leave.

Had it not been for her desire to see her godfather before he left, she would have pleaded a headache and stayed in her room. But knowing he would think she was ill if she did not make an effort to be with him and, reluctant to have him worry about her, she went downstairs.

As she had supposed, he was by the pool, a favorite meeting place for most of the guests who came to stay with the Khans. Equally expected was the sight of Karim lounging beside him. Their shining wet hair told her they had been swimming, though they now wore cool cotton robes like djellabas. It was unnerving to see Karim in the daylight, and she started to tremble. Briefly her glance rested on him before moving quickly away to Desmond who drew her down to sit beside him.

"All dressed up," he commented. "Aren't you going in for a swim?"

"I have a slight headache; I slept badly."

"You do look peaky."

The very Englishness of the word brought quick tears to her eyes, and she was glad that her sunglasses hid them, though she felt nothing could hide her feelings from Karim whose black stare seemed to pierce through her.

Without looking at him she could describe him perfectly and her feeling of helplessness grew. No man had the right to look so handsome. The loosely fitting white robe made his skin glow like bronze, while the water clinging to his hair gave it the appearance of black metal. It was disarranged, and she saw that in the last few weeks he had let it grow longer, which gave the ends a tendency to curl. Relaxed as he now was in the chair on the other side of her, he still had too much the look of a hunter ever to seem completely in repose, and she wondered if he had that same air of watchfulness about him when he slept. That was something she would never know. Hurriedly she shifted her position, trying to block out her view of him. But she could still see his long body and the strong muscular legs which tapered down to well-arched feet. Again she had the impression of a coiled spring. But it was not one that would snap under strain. This was a spring that would grow tighter and tighter before suddenly uncoiling itself with a shattering strength.

"A swim might do your headache good." Karim spoke. for the first time, his voice hauntingly soft, as if the words were meant only for her ears.

"I may go in later when the sun goes down," she murmured.

"You mean after we've left for Teheran and can't see you?" Amusement added depth to his tone and he looked in Desmond's direction. "Fleur doesn't like me to see her in a swimsuit. Don't you find that surprising?"

"Very much so since she's a champion swimmer." Desmond regarded her. "Surely Karim isn't right?"

"Of course, he isn't." Irritation made it possible to look at Karim without the fear that her love for him would give her away. She hoped he would go on saying things to annoy her. If he did, it might enable her to get through the rest of the week without giving herself away. "I swim a great deal when I have the pool to myself, but I don't think it's right for me to use it when there are guests around."

"You are a guest, too," Karim said.

"I'm here as Nizea's teacher."

"We invited you here to keep her company," he said flatly.

"You can play with words as much as you like, Mr. Khan, but you won't make me change my mind."

"Spoken like a true woman," he teased and, getting to his feet, slipped off his robe and walked to the edge of the pool.

Like a rabbit fascinated by a stoat, Fleur could not take her eyes away from the muscles that rippled across the bronze shoulders. How narrow-waisted and slim-hipped he was, yet what strength he emanated. He raised his arms and for an instant his biceps bulged. Then he dived into the water, clean as a knife in butter, and cleaved his way through it to the far end.

"He's a handsome man," Desmond said softly, "and a great worry to his father."

She could not talk about either of the Khan men and so

remained silent. But it didn't worry the man beside her who seemed intent on his own thoughts.

"Of course, I can see why Ibrahim Khan wants to get him married. He's the only son and until he produces an heir—several heirs, in fact—there'll be no one to carry on the name."

"I suppose that still matters out here?" she said with an effort.

"It matters to every family where there's money and power."

She knew she had to say something and, because the question of Karim's marriage held a fascination for her, she remained with it.

"He seems such a dutiful son to me that I'm surprised he hasn't done as his father wanted years ago. Thirty-two is quite old for a Persian to be single."

"Karim's a law unto himself—the way Ibrahim was before him. Besides, he's spent many years in the States and England. I often doubted whether he would be able to come back and settle here, but he's managed it extremely well."

"Extremely well," she said, remembering the way he had acquiesced to his father's attitude toward Nizea.

Karim was now swimming back to them, and she averted her eyes as he climbed out of the pool and came over to don his robe. The water gleaming on his skin emphasized its satiny texture, and she could almost sense how smooth it would be to the touch. He pulled his robe around him, then slipped his feet into leather sandals.

"If you'll excuse me," he said in an unusually crisp tone, "I have some things to attend to before lunch." He glanced in Fleur's direction. "As you have a headache, I suggest you come back to the house. You will find it cooler."

"I'm quite cool here." Through her dark glasses she looked at him, wishing she wore mirrored ones which would make it impossible for him to see her eyes.

"It will still be better if you come inside." He put out his hand. "Come."·

"I prefer to remain here."

"Very well." He gave no sign of discomfiture and, with a casual smile, walked away.

"Karim isn't used to having his women disobey him," Desmond smiled. "I thought he took it rather well."

"I'm not one of his women."

"You are living in the Khan home and you come into his orbit. That qualifies you as one! Don't fight it, my dear. Most Persian men of his type have the same protective manner towards women."

"You're generalizing, Professor," she teased.

"So I am." He appeared faintly discomfited. "That's a particularly stupid thing to do where Karim is concerned. He isn't a man one should generalize about. I'd never like to hazard a guess how he'd react to any given situation, because he's likely to do the exact opposite."

"Except where tradition is concerned," Fleur said. "Then he acts true to form." Her godfather eyed her curiously, and she knew she would have to explain what she meant. "I was thinking of Nizea. I'm sure if he had stood up for her, his father might have been persuaded to change his mind."

"How do you know he didn't try? He'd be the last person to admit to any disagreement between himself and his father. Anyway, she could well be far happier if she remains within her family's influence. She is a high-strung girl . . ."

"She's very level-headed."

"Only if you judge her by European standards. Considering how restricted her upbringing has been, she's remarkably uninhibited. Let the Khans do as they think best, Fleur, and don't interfere."

"I've no intention of trying. I told them how I feel, and I've left it at that."

She settled back in her chair. It was good to talk to someone like Desmond. He reduced all contention to its basic difference, stripping away the fripperies of pretense and disclosing the bare bones. She wished she could ask his opinion of her own situation but knew she dare not mention it. Last night Karim had been overcome by emotion. In the clarity of daylight he would see his passion for what it was and recognize its foolishness. To discuss it with her godfather would give it a credibility it did not have.

"Is anything wrong?" Desmond's mild voice broke into her thoughts and she shifted in her seat and regarded him.

"Of course not. I've just got a headache."

"I wasn't thinking of your headache. Merely that you seem tense and unlike yourself."

"It's the climate," she hedged. "I find it very enervating."

"But otherwise you don't regret coming to Iran?"

What would he say if she told him she regretted it bitterly and that her brief stay here had marked her life forever?

"I'm enjoying every minute of it," she lied. "It's like living in another world."

"It is another world. You would do well to remember that."

Something in the way he spoke made her search his face. There was no change in his expression, and she decided it was safer not to question him. In his own quiet way he was giving her a warning and hoping that if she saw it as such, she would pay heed to it. But she did not need anyone to warn her not to fall in love with a man like Karim Khan. She knew that for herself.

How self-assured Karim had been when he had asked her to go back with him to the house. She remembered the way his eyes had flashed when she had refused and knew that ahead of her lay an unpleasant meeting with him. What unkind fate had brought her to the Khans' summer home and made her virtually a prisoner here? Had she been in Teheran she could have avoided seeing him after last night. Yet it was not having to see him that worried her so much as the explanation she would have to give, for Karim would use all his persuasive powers to prevent her from turning him down. He would try to make her believe she was wrong; urge her to consider their love for one another. Her breath caught in her throat. He had never used the word "love"; only the word "want." And there was a world of difference between the two.

She swung her feet to the ground and stood up. "I must go and see Nizea. Do come and talk to her, Uncle Desmond. I'd like her to show you some of her stories."

"Fine. I didn't even know she was interested in literature until Ibrahim told me about it. He seemed quite proud of her."

"But not proud enough," Fleur said bitterly.

"Now, now," her godfather warned, putting his arms across her shoulders as they walked back to the house. "I thought I told you not to get involved in family matters."

As they entered the hall they saw Nizea being carried downstairs by one of the servants.

"Dahlia Sadeh and her family are coming to lunch," she explained, naming a friend from school.

"That will be fun for you." Fleur was pleased, for Dahlia was a sweet girl. "I didn't realize her family were friendly with yours."

"They're hoping for even stronger links," Nizea said with a swift glance into the salon where servants were circulating among a few of the guests who had already arrived. "My father is anxious for Karim to marry Dahlia's sister, Ferada, but at the moment he still prefers his freedom. I think he . . ."

"Let the servant put you down," Fleur interrupted. "You're heavy for him to keep carrying."

"I'll let him take me into the salon. But go up and change and hurry back down."

Once more Fleur mourned her godfather's presence here, for now she was forced again to enter into a family occasion she would have preferred to avoid. She was not surprised to learn there was one particular girl whom Ibrahim Khan wanted his son to marry. From her knowledge of Middle Eastern customs, she knew that the marriage of a son, particularly when he was the sole heir to a considerable fortune, was a matter of great importance and not undertaken lightly. For the Khans in particular, the girl would have to fulfill many requirements—suitable family and financial endowment being the two most important. From what she knew of Karim, the girl would also have to be beautiful and, coming unobserved into the salon a little later, this last belief was aptly confirmed.

The girl had the full, yet delicate beauty often seen in ancient Persian miniatures. Her face was a classical oval with large, doelike eyes, a small full mouth, and a thin, slightly long nose with finely arched nostrils. Her hair was black and lustrous, like that of most of her country-women, though she wore it in an extremely sophisticated style: parted in the center and waving on either side of her face before being drawn on to the nape of her neck and held there in a pearl spangled net. She was as exquisitely formed as a ballerina and walked with the same grace. But her smile was gay and uninhibited and animated her face each time she looked up at Karim who was standing beside her. Though she did not touch him Fleur had the impression that the girl was intensely conscious of his nearness. But then what woman wouldn't be?

"So there you are," he said to Fleur and came across to her, lowering his voice appreciably. "I was watching for you. Why didn't you come back to the house with me earlier? I wanted to talk to you."

"I thought you had things to do," she said, avoiding his eyes.

"Didn't you know that was an excuse? You were trying to avoid me—I know that—but you won't succeed."

"Please," she whispered, "leave me alone. People are watching us."

"You won't always be able to use them as an excuse."

Nonetheless, he stepped away from her, and she noticed with wry bitterness that he did not suggest introducing her to the girl to whom he was returning. She glanced round and, seeing her godfather in the corner talking to a group of people, went over to join him, stopping on the way to accept one of the delicious fruit drinks that were always served on these occasions.

The salon was now full of people, and their voices echoed in the airy lightness of the room. As usual everyone was impeccably dressed, with none of the casualness that would have been the norm on a similar occasion in England. Even in a country house in the height of summer, there was no relaxation from formal attire, and the men wore perfectly cut suits in lightweight material while the women resembled jeweled butterflies.

Fleur knew her coloring made her stand out among them. Her sleepless night might have increased the pallor of her creamy skin, but it had not diminished the vibrancy of the red-gold hair that framed her face.

To emphasize the fact that she did not consider herself a guest here, she wore one of her usual shirtwaisters. It was a pale lilac with a soft, standing collar and long sleeves casually rolled back to the elbows. The very casualness of the style suited her tall slenderness, as did the narrow circlet of shining gold around her neck and the simple gold sandals on her feet. She presented a picture of studied elegance that was more apparent because of its simplicity, and many appreciative male eyes observed her as she stood chatting to Desmond.

To her discomfiture Ibrahim Khan joined them, and the talk veered to politics, which was always a topic of conversation where men were gathered. Fleur had her own opinion of the world situation but knew better than to voice it here, and it was not until Desmond Anderson deliberately drew her into the discussion that she gave it.

"You have a very decided view of the economy," an older Persian man said to her.

"Only of worldwide economy. I wouldn't presume to comment on Iran's handling of its finances."

"Then you are a diplomat too!"

"That's a necessity when one is in a foreign country."

There were smiles at this, but before the conversation could resume, Madame Khan, resplendent in a vivid caftan, marshaled her guests onto the terrace. Here small tables were set for parties of six, and servants were already gliding between them, bearing the usual silver dishes piled with food.

"You're sitting with me." Desmond led her to the nearest table.

Unfortunately it gave her a direct view of Karim who was holding out a chair for Ferada, before taking his place beside her. His whole attention was focused on the girl, and because his lids were lowered it made his expression difficult to read. But then, Fleur thought bitterly, she had always found it impossible to know what he was thinking. Only for a brief moment last night, when he had held her in his arms, had it been all too clear.

"It would be an excellent match," Desmond said softly, as if he knew where her attention lay. "Mr. Sadeh is an important lawyer and is anxious to branch out internationally. With Karim as his son-in-law, it would be much easier."

"I'd hate to be married for commercial reasons," Fleur muttered, "particularly if I were as beautiful as Ferada."

"Today you are more beautiful," Desmond murmured, giving her a fatherly smile. "But I grant you she's a lovely creature."

Fleur tried to ignore the Persian girl and concentrate on her godfather and the man on the other side of her. He was the owner of an art gallery, and the conversation soon ranged over all aspects of modern art. She enjoyed nothing better than a lively argument, and the verbal pyrotechnics at their table caused several nearby guests to still their own conversation in order to listen.

It was the sudden silence around her that made Fleur realize she was the center of attraction on this part of the terrace, and she grew hot with embarrassment and wished she could lift up the tablecloth and hide beneath it.

"Why didn't you stop me from prattling on?" she besought Desmond.

"Because I like it when you let off steam."

She pulled a face and, half turning, saw Karim lean forward to light a cigarette for the girl next to him. She had never seen him smoke and was surprised he carried a lighter. He used it with the ease of practice and for a moment kept his fingers lightly on the Persian girl's slender hand.

Fleur set her fork sharply on her plate. It was unnerving to be so affected by a man she barely knew. It was only six weeks since she had met him, and she had not spoken to him more than half a dozen times nor been alone with him for more than three of them. Yet their attraction for each other had been strong from the beginning. There was no point in pretending otherwise.

What was it that made two people want each other? In her case it could only stem from physical desire. Ideologically they were poles apart. She believed women had a sixth sense, an intuition that gave them heightened perception, but perhaps there was a seventh sense that made them aware when the right man came along? Perhaps that accounted for the emotion Karim aroused in her. But regardless of how she felt, she had to escape him. Escape and think.

Her eyes roamed the room. Ibrahim Khan was sitting some distance away but almost as if he had received a signal, he shifted in his chair and fixed his gaze on her. All she could see of him was the beige suit he wore, which made his beard look magnificently dark, but she felt his power and was afraid of it.

"I wish I could go back to Teheran with you," she said impulsively to Desmond. "I'm getting claustrophobic staying here."

"Then fly back with me for a few days."

Remembering Karim was taking him, she shook her head.

"Why not?" her godfather pressed. "Karim told me this morning he's staying on here, so there'll be plenty of room. And you can return the day after tomorrow when the helicopter comes back to collect the Khans."

It was too good an opportunity to miss. She would have to return, of course, but at least it would get her away for a couple of days and give her a chance to think clearly.

"What time are you leaving?" she asked.

"In about an hour."

"Then I'll go and get ready and have a word with Mrs. Khan. I can't dash off without permission."

When she spoke to her hostess as she escorted her female guests into one of the many cool sitting-rooms that overlooked the garden, she received an immediate yes.

"You are free to come and go as you please, Miss Peters. There is no question of your having to obtain our permission. In fact, my husband commented only this morning that he thought you looked tired. A change will do you good."

With a murmur of agreement Fleur hurried off to pack a few things. She had to pass through the main salon to reach the hall and was halfway across it when a group of guests came in from the terrace. Karim was among them, towering head and shoulders above his shorter compatriots. He saw her at once and reached her in three long strides.

"What's this I hear about your going to Teheran?"

"I need a break."

"But I stayed behind because of you. You can't run away from me."

"I'm not running away."

"You are! You've been avoiding me all day."

Involuntarily her eyes slid to Ferada who was standing by the window looking in their direction. Karim did not follow Fleur's gaze though the tightening of his mouth told her he knew she was looking at the Persian girl.

"You have no need to be jealous of any other woman," he stated flatly.

"I'm not." The soft tendrils of hair on Fleur's forehead clung damply to her skin, and she pushed them away with her hand.

Karim caught his breath. "How beautiful you are! I'm aching to hold you—to kiss you." He bent closer. "You can't go to Teheran. You must stay here."

"You have no right to give me orders."

"I'm not giving you orders. I'm begging you to do as I ask."

Her longing to obey was so strong that only by maintaining her anger against him could she say no. Deliberately she looked at Ferada, knowing jealousy was her best self-defense and finding it flaming high as she saw the possessive way the girl was eying Karim.

"Did you hear what I said?" he demanded. "I'm begging you to stay here."

"I can't. I've already promised to go."

"Tell Desmond you've changed your mind. He'll understand."

She knew he would and searched for another excuse. If she herself was blindly jealous over Ferada, then Karim—a man with a strong possessive streak—would be equally jealous of any man who came between him and the one he wanted.

"I'm . . . I'm meeting a friend," she lied. "I can't let him down."

"Rory Baines?"

Amazed he had remembered the name, when she couldn't even remember telling it to him, she nodded.

"Then I won't try to dissuade you," he said curtly and immediately strode toward the Persian girl.

Trying to quell her bitterness, Fleur hurried away. How had she expected Karim to behave when she had told him she was going to Teheran to meet another man? Had she hoped he would force her to stay here, or had she expected him to call her bluff and say he would accompany her? If he had done that, he would have ruined her objective in going.

"But I wanted him to ruin it," she whispered as she entered her bedroom and, with these words, finally acknowledged to herself the depth of her love for him.

Nine

IT was not until the helicopter approached Teheran that Fleur felt an uplift of spirit and knew she had done the right thing in getting away for a few days.

No longer part of the Khan household, she could plan her future, though she was still not sure whether it should include remaining with Madame Nadar for the rest of her contract. As long as she stayed in Iran she would find it impossible to forget Karim. Only in England, surrounded by more prosaic and familiar things, would she become more aware of his exotic foreignness and be glad she had resisted it.

It was late afternoon when she reached Madame Nadar's house, having said good-bye to her godfather and declined his offer to dine with him. She was not sure if he were seeing Karim before he flew back to England and she didn't want to run the risk of his saying he had taken her out when she wanted Karim to believe she had been with Rory.

The thought of Rory prompted her to telephone him and the warmth in his voice gave her unexpected pleasure. Dear Rory, how good it was to have someone on whom she could rely. But as she greeted him in the school waiting-room later that evening, she could not help feeling guilty at using him in this way.

"It's a good thing you rang me when you did," he said, guiding her out to his car. "Another half hour and I'd have been on my way to the Club for a bridge tournament."

"You don't mean I prevented you from entering?"

"You certainly did, I'm delighted to say! I'd much rather see you than play cards." In the dusk he bent his head to peer into her face. "I expected to see you blooming, instead of which you look a bit wilted. Finding the Khans difficult to cope with?"

"I don't have to cope with them," she said. "I spend my time with Nizea."

"But you live *en famille,* don't you?"

She nodded and slipped into the front seat of the car. "I still feel guilty at preventing you from entering the tournament."

"I'll let you buy me a silver cup instead!" he grinned. "Or I'll settle for a spot of lovemaking."

She smiled at him briefly but her heart gave an uncomfortable lurch. However, her fears disappeared as the evening wore on, for he was an easy companion. There was no difficulty talking to him and no need to wonder whether she was saying something that might lead to a disagreement. How unlike her conversations with Karim, in which she had always been conscious of their divergent views on everything of importance.

"I can't tell you how wonderful it is to have you here," Rory said. "Having you fly down just to see me. Well, it's knocked me for a loop."

"I didn't just come to see you," she said hastily. "I had a few errands to do in Teheran."

"But you're still glad to see me?"

"Of course."

"How glad?" He leaned close. "You wouldn't . . . I mean there's no chance of your changing your mind about me, is there?"

"No." Her answer was emphatic, and color flooded her face as she saw his expression. "I'm sorry, Rory, but it's better for me to be honest."

"Oh, sure. I knew it was a long shot, but I still go on hoping."

"I wish you wouldn't. I'd feel much less guilty if we didn't see each other again."

"I hardly see you anyway. Besides, I've no intention of being in Teheran and not seeing you. I'm interested in your well-being and, so long as you're living in a city of foreigners, I'm going to take care of you."

"I'm not living in a city of foreigners," she laughed. "They belong here—we're the foreigners."

He laughed, too, and then raised his glass.

"I've nothing to celebrate, but I guess that's the time when one should. So drink up, and let's dance."

The ease with which Rory had taken his refusal did not fool Fleur. She knew him well enough to sense his hurt, and she admired the kindness that made him pretend otherwise. It made her refuse to see him the following day, despite his insistence that he didn't want things to change between them.

"Things have to change between us," she said. "You are far too eligible to waste all your free time on me."

His protestations remained with her as she undressed and climbed into bed. But as she lay back on the pillows and looked out at the patch of sky that she could see through the window, his voice was superseded by Karim's melodic one. How furious he had been when she had left him that afternoon, but how quickly he had turned to Ferada. Was that the course his actions would take in the future? With all her heart she hoped it was, for if he were married he would no longer wish to lay siege to her own heart.

It was all too easy to see Ferada as his wife. The girl was beautiful and, from the little Nizea had said about her, lived a purely social life, which would please Karim much more than having a wife who followed her own career. *I could never be happy with him,* she thought, and tried to concentrate on this, hoping to lessen the grief she felt at knowing she had never been given the chance. The love he had offered her would never have included a simple band of gold. Diamonds and a back-street affair, more likely.

Angrily she sat up and switched on the lamp. She was becoming maudlin and thinking like an Edwardian heroine. Affairs today were not conducted in a back street but in the full glare of public knowledge. Even in Teheran Karim would have treated their liaison as an open secret. *For heaven's sake, stop thinking of Karim,* she told herself and reached for a book. Unfortunately, it was the verses of Omar Khayyam and, knowing they would not serve to distract her but have the opposite effect, she searched in the drawer until she found a dog-eared murder story that belonged to one of the other teachers. Perhaps in trying to solve a crime she would be able to forget the crime she had committed in allowing herself to fall in love with a man she could not have. Recollecting the ardor with which he had looked at her, she knew it was all too easy to have him. The trouble was that it would have to be on his terms. She opened the book and, seeing her ringless hand, mourned the indoctrination which made it impossible for her to love freely outside the bonds of marriage.

In the morning she awoke feeling depressed and knew that activity was the only way of overcoming it. But the school was empty of pupils and teachers, and Madame Nadar was spending several weeks in Paris with friends, leaving only the servants in the house.

For a short while she did some sketching in the garden. Then, remembering her mother's dictum that there was nothing like buying a hat to make one feel better, she decided to take herself to the bazaar district. Telling one of the servants not to set lunch for her, since she was not sure what time she would be back, she set off.

Teheran had grown enormously in the last ten years, but it still adhered to the Islamic rule that business should be centered in a single place, with trades rigidly segregated. The bazaar reflected this though several toyshops and ironmongers had started to infiltrate the jewelry and material stores. However, in the side streets the segregation of the trades was maintained more effectively, with a whole area given over to metalworkers who produced intricately inlaid articles in gold, silver and bronze; there was a grocery area as well as an Armenian section, which appeared to consist of wine and spirit merchants. But even here Fleur knew that progress was swiftly changing things. Teheran was spreading northward, and businesses would move with it, leaving whole sections of the southern part of the bazaar abandoned.

The streets were thick with people; families shopping together and separate groups of women and men, all intent on spending their money and getting the most for it. The majority of the shops were tiny and single-storied, their interiors often so dark that one had to bring things out into the daylight to see them properly. Her original intention of buying some costume jewelry had to be abandoned, for she hated bargaining and knew that unless she did, she would be grossly overcharged.

After an hour of indecision she left the bazaar and headed for Loear Street. Here was shopping on a more sophisticated level, and though she would have to pay more than in the bazaar, she knew she would be getting value for money.

But the jewelry—even the simpler pieces—was too expensive to be bought as casual gifts, and the fabrics she liked were breathtakingly expensive—sufficient brocade to make a simple dress being enough to set her back a month's salary. But she was not going to return from her expedition empty-handed, and she eventually bought a bracelet—of heavy silver inset with blue stones—and a small, brass and enamel lamp which she knew her mother would love to hang in their hall in Surrey. The thought of home made her nostalgic and increased the vulnerability she had felt since she had admitted her love for Karim.

It was three o'clock when her taxi, which she had shared with several other people—a custom common in the city—deposited her at Madame Nadar's. She was tired and hot and longing for a drink. Balancing her two parcels in one hand, she unlocked the gate and walked through the garden to the house.

This time tomorrow she would have to go to the airport to meet the helicopter that would be bringing Ibrahim Khan and his son to Teheran. With a modicum of luck she might be able to avoid talking to Karim and, by the time he returned to the country, she would have left the house permanently. It was a pity her association with Madame Nadar made it impossible for her to leave the Khans without giving them time to make suitable arrangements for someone else to act as Nizea's companion. She moistened her lips. It was odd that Mr. Khan had chosen her when there must have been any number of girls of Nizea's own age who would have been delighted to keep her company. She remembered his knowing look as he had gazed at her the night before last and was sure he regretted having brought her into his home. Poor Mr. Khan. She should have assured him she had no designs upon his son. But even if she had, he might not have believed her.

The hall was almost as warm as the garden, for when she was abroad Madame Nadar insisted on strict economy and would not allow her servants to use the air conditioning. In England, no domestic help would have remained with her under such conditions but here, where jobs were still at a premium and illiteracy so high that domestic work was frequently the only occupation for many men and women, they had to accept poor conditions.

An elderly servant in a long blue shift shuffled forward. The garment enveloped her from head to toes, and she held a corner of it in her hand to hide her face. She motioned behind her with her other hand and Fleur looked in the direction of the waiting-room whose door, beyond the recess of an archway, was still closed.

"Is it someone to see me?" she asked and, as the woman nodded, ruefully knew that Rory still intended to pursue her.

Still holding her packages she pushed open the waiting-room door and went in. But the tall man with the glittering black eyes who stood in the center of the room glaring at her, was a far cry from the pleasant-faced one she had expected to see.

"You!" she gasped.

"Disappointed?" he questioned icily.

"Yes," she said irritably, "I am."

She went over to a table by the window and placed her two parcels on it.

"I didn't think you and your father would be arriving until tomorrow," she went on. "I was planning to meet the helicopter in the afternoon and go back with the pilot."

"So you do intend to come back?" he said harshly. "I wondered whether it was your intention to remain here and ask us to send on your clothes."

It was an idea that had not occurred to her and, momentarily, she wished it had.

"I find I have to come back to Teheran earlier than I

had anticipated," she said carefully. "But I wouldn't . . .
I would remain with Nizea until it was convenient for me
to leave."

"And what about *my* convenience?"

Her head rose sharply and with it her temper. "I don't
see that your convenience enters into it."

"Don't you?" he asked and muttered something in his
own language.

She knew little Persian but his tone made it clear that,
if his words had color, the air around him would have
been decidedly blue.

"Are you willfully playing dumb?" he demanded. "Or
do you wish me to believe you don't love me? How dare
you say I shouldn't be concerned with whether you go or
stay in my parents' home? Didn't I make it clear to you
the other night that I want you to be mine? Didn't you lie
in my arms and return my kisses?"

"Hardly," she said shakily. "As far as I remember, you
held me by force."

"Only because I knew you were afraid and wanted to
run from me. But once I overcame your fears . . ." He
took a step toward her, stopping as he saw the way she
tensed. "You did return my kisses," he said huskily, "and
you do love me. I saw it in your eyes then, and I see it in
your eyes now. The way you can see it in mine if only
you will look into them."

This was the last thing she wanted to do, and she
swung round to the window, giving him a view of her
slender back and the heavy fall of red-gold hair.

"I don't know what you're hoping to prove by all this,"
she said. "But even if I . . . I did kiss you back, it was

only because you're an . . . an attractive man. Anyway, a kiss doesn't mean much these days."

"Ours did."

"No," she said sharply. "It won't work. I'm not going to have a love affair with you. The sooner you accept that, the easier it will be for both of us."

His step was quick across the tiled floor as he came to stand directly behind her. Then his hands were heavy on her shoulders as he pulled her roughly round to face him. "Is that what you think I want?"

Since she could not avoid looking at him, she faced him directly. "I don't blame you for it. You're handsome and intelligent and obviously used to having a lot of affairs. But I'm not. It's old-fashioned of me, I know, but . . ."

"I don't need you to tell me that you're a virgin."

She lowered her eyelids. He gave the word such a tender quality that it immediately conjured up erotic images in her mind. She tried to dismiss them but while he was holding her it was impossible.

"If you . . . if you know that," she whispered, "then you can understand why I don't want . . ."

"I'm not asking you to have an affair with me. I thought you'd know that without my telling you." His hand dropped away from her, and his eyes had the sharpness of a bird of prey. "Do you think I'm the sort of man who would debase the woman I love by suggesting such a relationship? I know how lightly sex is regarded in the West but here, when a man loves a woman the way I love *you*, he thinks only of sharing his whole life with her; of giving her his name; of having her bear his children. I'm talking of marriage, Fleur. I want you to be my wife."

She swayed against the table. "No. It's impossible."

"Because I don't have the pale face and blond hair of your English boy friend?"

"It's got nothing to do with that!"

"What then?"

"We're different—in other ways. You can't want to marry me. It's only physical attraction."

"Is that all you feel for *me?*"

He reached out for her and pulled her close. Heat emanated from him and the pale gray linen suit he wore was faintly damp. There was a sheen across his forehead and upper lip, but she knew it was not caused by the stultifying atmosphere so much as the tense emotion rising within him.

"Answer me, Fleur," he grated. "When I hold you like this, do you feel only desire? Does your heart tell you nothing else?"

"It doesn't matter how I feel," she cried. "It wouldn't work. You saw me in your home. You must know that for yourself."

"I know only that you fit into my arms as if you were made for them and that I will hold no other woman."

She tried to resist what he was saying, but her head felt light as thistledown, blown hither and thither by the intensity of his words.

"I know all your doubts," he rasped. "Mine were equally strong, but I was able to overcome them. When a man loves a woman the way I love you, differences of race and religion cease to matter. We are two people who have found each other, and we cannot part."

Putting his hands on either side of her head he rested his mouth upon hers. It was not the passionate kiss of two nights ago but one of gentleness. His lips were soft and warm and the tip of his tongue came out and gently ran along the side of her mouth and across her cheek. Only then did he give a muffled exclamation and bury his face in the fragrant cloud of her hair. Twining his fingers in it, he pushed the strands aside to find the shell-like ear lobe.

"I love you," he whispered. "We will be so happy together, heart of my heart."

"No, Karim." She tried to push him away, but his strength was too much for her. "It won't work," she repeated. "What you're saying is impossible."

"It's impossible for me to live without you," he replied. "Why are you fighting me so?"

Still holding her tightly, he turned her face until their eyes met. She had never been so near to them, and she saw they were not black, as she had imagined, but rich brown in a milky blue sea and framed by amazingly long lashes. Then his eyes came nearer still, going out of focus as his mouth claimed hers again. This time there was desire in his kiss and in the hands that caressed her. Her own desire rose, and her lips parted to allow him entry. She could no more have denied him than the sky could have refused passage to the sun, and she gave him back kiss for kiss, caress for caress, savoring each moment as if it were her last. She was spent when he finally lifted his head and he, too, looked dazed.

"You see what we do to each other?" he said hoarsely. "How can you say you don't love me?" His fingertips traced her eyebrows and moved along her temple. "Tell me you love me, Fleur. I have waited so long to hear it."

"Not all that long," she protested, still terribly unwilling to make this final confession. "We haven't been alone together more than three or four times. We hardly know each other. You don't know the way I feel . . . only the way I look."

"I know that when you speak my name with your soft, precise voice, I feel as if you are dancing on my spine!"

"Be serious," she protested. "You know what I'm trying to say."

"And *I* am trying to tell you that you're worrying over nothing. Of course there's much I don't know about you. Equally, there are many things you don't know about me. But that's the way it should be between a man and a woman until they are married." His breath was warm on her cheek as his head came low again. "Once you are mine, there'll be no secrets between us."

Fleur did not know whether to laugh or cry. She was deliriously happy to hear that Karim wanted to marry her, that he did not wish to hide his love for her, yet she was afraid that their happiness could not last. She did not share his belief that marriage would nullify their differences. He had too many ties, too many other loyalties that would pull him apart from her. Tears poured down her cheeks and, as he felt them on his skin, he lifted her up into his arms and carried her across to a settee. He sat down and held her on his lap. He was so big that she felt like a child, though the stirring of his body told her he did not regard her that way. Pink-cheeked, she hid her face in his chest, her hands moving inside his jacket to come around his back. It was frightening the way her need of this man could supersede her coolness of mind and make her a stranger to herself. She might say she could never love Karim without marriage but, if he wanted to take possession of her, she knew she didn't have the strength to resist him. More than that—she wanted to encourage him. With a half cry she pulled away from him and stared up into his face.

"We can't get married, Karim. It wouldn't work. Be logical about it."

"I have used my logic for nights without number. I have walked my room from dusk till dawn and counted the cost of what I plan to do. But all along I knew I was fighting a hopeless battle. I am nothing without you, Fleur. You are my happiness and my life."

The poetry of his words thrilled her. But at the same time it illustrated his foreignness and made her see him as an alien with whom she would never feel at home.

"You . . . you think that now," she said hesitatingly, "but you might change your mind in the future."

"Only when the stars fall from the sky," he said whimsically and, rising from the settee and still holding her, deposited her in a chair a few yards away. Then he went back to the settee and sat down. "Now we can talk with the logic you demand. When I am close to you I can think of nothing except how much I want you."

He crossed one long leg over the other and then remained still. It made her realize he was not a man given to nervous gestures. Everything he did was precise and carefully thought out, as befitted a man of law. She clutched at the thought. Karim was a lawyer with a Western education that would at least give them a meeting point. But no, she mustn't think in this way, for then she would stop seeing him as an alien and have no need to fight him.

"I know you think I'm old-fashioned in many ways," he said, "but much that I do is done out of respect for my father who is an old man. Were I alone and free to do as

I wish, many things would be different." He paused for an instant. "My sister, for example. I would not prevent her from going to the university."

"You could at least have said so."

"To what avail? I am not prepared to fight my father over it, and to cause discord for nothing . . ."

"But are you prepared to fight him over me? Or does he approve of your wanting to marry me?"

The beautifully molded face of the man took on a shuttered look. The eyes became opaque, closing off all their expression, and the features tautened, making it impossible to know what was going on in the quick mind behind the smooth, high forehead.

"Your father is a man of the old school," Fleur continued, knowing here was her only chance of making Karim see reason. "He'll never be happy for you to have a Western wife. He wants you to marry someone like Ferada Sadeh."

"That's true," Karim agreed, his face still a mask that denied all expression. "But there comes a time when a man—even a devoted son like myself—must be his own master. When my father realizes the way I feel about you, he will accept you."

Fleur did not agree with him but knew it was pointless to say so. Only by believing in what he was saying could Karim continue to beg her to be his wife.

"Darling, don't look so distressed." He uncrossed his legs and placed his hands on them as he leaned towards her. "In the beginning it won't be easy—I grant you that—but when my parents see how happy I am with you, they will love you as if they had chosen you themselves."

Fleur knew it would be nice to believe this and nicer

still to be as sure that she could make Karim happy. But she was uncertain of her ability to meet the needs of this demanding man. Uncertain and also unwilling. Did she really want a life where her every action had to be pre-meditated lest it go against custom and raise a few eye-brows? Did she want a husband who, from his earliest youth, had been brought up to believe that women were inferior beings put on earth to serve their masters? Fear caught at her throat as if it had hands, and she gasped.

"What is it?" he demanded and came swiftly to her side. He knelt on the floor and brought his face level with hers.

"I'm afraid," she whispered. "Our lives have been so different. We have no common meeting ground. We may love each other but every time we're alone we quarrel."

"Because we're uncertain of each other." His voice was firm with assurance, though a faint smile quirked one side of his mouth. "Anyway, you are the one who does the quarreling—not I." He put his fingers against her lips to stop her speaking. "Once you are my wife, you won't feel the need to express yourself in the same way."

"I could never be subservient," she said, pushing away his hand. "You can't turn me into a puppet in a yash-mak!"

Astonished, he looked at her, then he broke into a chuckle. Suddenly he became much younger and less frightening. "Nor do I wish to turn you into a doll in a wimple!"

"Wimples went out of fashion centuries ago."

"So did the harem and the yashmak. Not centuries, perhaps, but far enough back for you not to worry about it." His grin became wicked. "Besides, I wouldn't fancy you if you were docile. It's your sharp tongue and quick mind that I love, not just the fragile body and full breasts."

Instantly her hands came up to cover them, and he rose to his feet. "You won't always be shy of me, my lovely English flower. Soon you will unfold the inner sweetness to me."

Her hands fluttered more urgently, wanting to remain where they were and also wanting to hide her burning cheeks. Because she could not do both she gave an embarrassed laugh. "I do find your compliments unnerving. I . . . I'm not used to them."

"I'm glad to hear it. I wouldn't like to think other men have the right to say such things to you! Which reminds me—did you see Rory Baines last night?"

"Yes." She paused. "He asked me to marry him."

Karim's expletive, though foreign, made his meaning clear, and she was thrilled by his jealousy.

"You refused him, of course?"

For a reason she could not understand, Fleur was reluctant to be completely honest and, a long time later, was to remember this with gratitude. "No. I . . . er . . . didn't. I told him I wasn't sure how I felt."

"Weren't sure how you felt?" Karim spat out the words as if they were poison. "Don't you know that you love *me*? That *I'm* the man you want to marry?" He pulled her so roughly to her feet that her arms were nearly jerked from their sockets. "You're mine, do you hear? I'll never let you belong to anyone else. Never. I'll kill you first!"

His expression—more than his words—told her he was not joking. But instead of dismaying her, she reveled in it, realizing that beneath her veneer of emancipation there lurked the primitive urge to be mastered. It made her feel a traitor to the cause of liberation for which she had fought all her life, and she knew that when she was away from this man she would hate herself for being so weak. But during their moments of togetherness, when they retreated from the world and were wholly absorbed in one another, she could not help herself.

Tentatively her hands came out and touched his hair, then moved down to the nape of his neck. "I do love you," she said huskily. "But I can't marry you."

"You can," he said confidently and, catching hold of her hands, kissed each one of her fingers. "I daren't touch your lips again, or I'll never be able to let you go, and the helicopter's waiting to take us out of this dreadful heat." He ran his free hand round the inside edge of his collar. "Is there no air conditioning here?"

"Madame Nadar doesn't have it on when she's away."

He muttered something unflattering, and Fleur smiled. "I'll be a couple of minutes packing."

"I'm tempted to come up with you," he said, opening the door for her. "But I won't," he added as he saw her quick look of alarm. "The heat has sapped away my strength, and I wouldn't be able to keep my distance from you."

"You make it sound as if you're fighting a battle."

"I am," he said gravely. "But it will lead to a very sweet victory."

Ten

N*EITHER of the Khans made any refer-*
ence to Fleur's return with their son and, when she spoke
to Karim alone later that night in the garden, he admitted
that he had told his father he had had to go to Teheran
on business and had collected her at the same time.

"My father didn't believe me," he said. "I'm sure he
knew I flew down in order to bring you back."

Fleur was equally sure Ibrahim Khan also believed that
his son only wanted to have an affair with her, but she
was too wise to say it. Karim was obstinate and could well
become intransigent in the face of opposition. This in turn
could lead him into marrying her, even against his own
better judgment.

"What stick are you beating yourself with now?" he
asked whimsically. "I can see the pain in your eyes."

"I was wondering if you'd have noticed me if I'd been

149

polite to you the first time we met," she lied, "or if it was only because I answered you back."

"If you'd had your tongue cut out I would have noticed you," he teased. "Don't you know how beautiful you are?"

"I try not to think about it, and I wish other people wouldn't."

"Why not?" His perfectly arched eyebrows drew together above his nose. "If one sees a magnificent painting, does one wish it was less magnificent? Or when you hear a wonderful symphony, do you want it to be played out of tune?"

"Symphonies and paintings don't change with time—the way looks do."

"Ah!" he said, understanding her. "You believe that since I love your beauty, my love for you will fade when you grow old."

"Won't it?"

He was silent for so long that she miserably concluded he could not find a diplomatic answer. She searched for something to say and her lips had parted when he suddenly spoke.

"A few hours ago you said there must have been many women who loved me because I was eligible and handsome. But have you ever wondered if their need for me would fade when my strength decreased and my hair grew gray?"

"It isn't the same for a man," she protested.

"You say that? You who want me to believe that men and women are equal? How do you know how a man feels when he flexes his muscles and only sees the movement of crepey skin? When he draws in his stomach and still it hangs down? Believe me, Fleur, men have as many fears as woman. Though I must admit that when I thought of my future with *you*, it never entered my mind to wonder if you would love me less at sixty-four than at thirty-two."

The idea of being with Karim so long seemed to dim her fears and make the future shine with a little more clarity. But it was still not clear enough for her to give the answer she knew he was waiting to hear. Her doubts were still strong and the differences between them too many.

The following day Karim and his father returned to Teheran, and Fleur made Nizea follow a more serious regime of study in the hope that it would take her own mind off her problems. But during every waking moment she kept thinking of Karim and, each time a servant came towards her, she wondered if it was to bring her a message from him. She had begged him not to telephone her, knowing they would be unable to talk without some servant overhearing and telling his mother, who would immediately inform her husband.

It was the thought of Ibrahim Khan that was making Fleur's decision more difficult. Indeed had it not been for him, she might have accepted Karim's proposal and the consequences be damned. But Ibrahim Khan was a man whose opinion she respected even though she did not always agree with it, for she knew him to be a man of sagacity who was frequently called upon to advise in a dispute. What advice would he give to her? She had little need to speculate. "Go back to your own country," he would say, "and marry your own kind."

On Thursday afternoon Fleur was in her room when

she heard Karim arrive. She knew from Nizea that father and son had spent a couple of days in Paris negotiating an important sale of antiques.

"It is only a hobby for my father," the girl had said. "Most of our fortune comes from financing imports and exports. And we have a great deal of property, too."

Fleur pretended an interest in some of the perfume bottles on Nizea's dressing-table. "I'm surprised your father didn't want your brother to join the family firm."

"My father was delighted when Karim elected to study law. He is a great believer in education—though only for men," the girl added bitterly.

"Well, your brother's certainly well-educated," Fleur said quickly, unwilling to have Nizea sink into self-pity again. "He went to Harvard as well as Oxford, didn't he?"

"Karim's brilliant," Nizea said matter-of-factly. "I'm not surprised all the girls are crazy about him." She stood up and walked gingerly to the door. The heavy cast on her leg had been replaced by a much lighter one, and she was still unused to the feel of it. "Don't you think I'm making good progress, Fleur?"

"Excellent," Fleur agreed and came forward to give Nizea her arm. "Hold on to me while we go downstairs. I'm not happy about your walking on these marble floors."

"I'm used to them. When I was a little girl Karim would hold me in his arms and pretend to skate on them. It was an advantage having a much older brother. He was like a very loving father."

But not sufficiently loving to defy his father in order to help you, Fleur thought but refrained from saying so.

Nizea's education was a subject she dared not discuss any more. It was depressing how much had to be held back if one wanted to keep the peace. She frowned at the knowledge, wondering what sort of future one could have if one was afraid to talk openly. Tonight she would tell this to Karim and see what he said. No doubt he would make light of it. If only he could succeed in helping her to make light of it too . . .

Unfortunately, she had no chance to talk with him alone that evening, for he came into the salon with his father only a few moments before dinner was served. Fleur still found it an ordeal to dine with the Khans. With Karim sitting opposite her it was difficult to prevent her need of him from shining out of her eyes, and she knew that her avoidance of him, either in making conversation or meeting his eyes, was almost as noticeable as if she had sat and gazed at him with admiration.

The conversation centered on their Paris trip. Nizea and her mother listened in silence and, on the couple of occasions when the older woman made a comment, it was only to agree with what her husband had said. Fleur had discovered her to be a woman completely dominated by her husband, a not really surprising fact since she was docile and he was aggressive. She had learned that the woman had married when she was sixteen and that Karim had been born a year later, which explained her youthful appearance.

"You are very quiet, Miss Peters." Ibrahim Khan interrupted her thoughts by signaling to one of the servants to offer her a selection of petits fours which he had brought back form Paris. "I hope you aren't homesick for England? Though it would be understandable if you were."

"I do miss my family," she acknowledged.

"Yet you voluntarily left them! I understand that Western women think it important to travel the world before they settle down and marry."

"Not all women think that marriage means settling down," Fleur smiled.

"Then why bother to get married? If you accept your husband's name, you accept the duty of looking after him and caring for his home."

In the face of such a statement Fleur could not hold her tongue. "I believe that a husband and wife agree to look after each other. Marriage is a partnership—not subservience for the woman."

"I had not realized you would regard taking care of your husband as being subservient to him."

Knowing the man was deliberately misunderstanding her—could it be his way of showing his son how wrong she was for him?—Fleur forced a guard upon her tongue and pretended to be absorbed in choosing another petit four.

"I presume you would also wish to continue with your career if you were married?" Ibrahim Khan persisted.

"I haven't given it any thought."

"But there's no reason why you shouldn't work. Luckily your compatriots hold the same views as you do. It is only here—in the Middle East—where the old traditions concerning women still exist."

"More's the pity," Nizea muttered. "Why shouldn't a woman have the same rights as a man?"

"Having rights—as you put it—does not necessarily make a woman happy."

"You think only a man can do that."

"A husband," her father corrected. "The right husband, of course."

"Chosen by her parents."

"Naturally." The wide lipped mouth, faintly seen beneath the thick beard, moved in a smile. "Look how happy your mother has been with her life."

"I'm not my mother."

"I think your father was generalizing," Fleur put in hastily.

Nizea was not to be placated and gave an angry toss of her head. But before she could say anything further, Karim took a small package from his breast pocket and tossed it across the table in her direction.

With a happy exclamation Nizea opened it to find three exquisite charms, each one set with a different jewel. There was a house with tiny emerald windows, a camel with sapphire eyes, and a ballerina with a ruby dotted skirt.

"Don't say I never think of you," Karim said. "It took me the best part of a morning to find those."

"During which time he kept me waiting an hour," Ibrahim Khan grumbled.

"You should be glad I went with you to Paris," Karim rejoined. "My partners are already complaining I spend more time on your affairs than I do on our company."

"It is your duty to look after your clients," his father pointed out.

"Even when that client refuses to pay his bill?" Karim was openly smiling. "What do you think of that, Mama?" he asked, turning his silky dark head in his mother's direction.

"I think you are a naughty boy to tease your father, but I will make sure he pays his bills immediately!"

Fleur enjoyed the unexpected banter, which lessened the tension she always experienced when dining with the family. But her edginess returned when they left the dining room for the salon. Mr. Khan settled himself in a beautifully carved chair that resembled a throne, while his wife sank gracefully onto a pile of cushions and picked up some embroidery on which she was working. Fleur looked at Nizea, hoping the girl would decide to go to her room, but instead she settled beside her mother.

"Come and sit next to me, Fleur," Karim called.

Fleur saw Ibrahim Khan's head turn sharply in her direction. "I—I'm fine here," she stammered and promptly took the nearest chair.

"We will be happy to excuse you if you wish to go to your room," Ibrahim Khan said majestically.

"As a matter of fact I do have some letters to write," Fleur said gratefully and went to rise.

"Stay where you are," Karim interrupted. "I don't wish you to leave us."

"Karim!" his father said sternly. "Miss Peters is a guest in our home. If she wishes to go to her room . . ."

"But she doesn't. She's only going there because she wants to run away."

"Don't you think you're being presumptuous in deciding what Miss Peters wishes to do?" his mother protested gently, pausing in her embroidery.

"I know exactly what Fleur wants to do—and why."

"I'm going to my room," Fleur said desperately and turned to the door.

As she moved she found her way barred by Karim

whose right hand shot out and caught hold of her wrist. "I think it's time we stopped pretending."

"Karim . . . please . . . let me go."

"How can I let go of something I've never had?" he asked with unexpected asperity.

"What's the matter with you, Karim?" his father demanded, his hands resting on the arms of his chair as if he were preparing to rise.

"Forgive me, Father." Karim still kept his grip on Fleur's hands. "But I'm tired of all this pretense. I think it's time you knew that I have asked Fleur to be my wife."

Fleur opened her mouth to protest but no sound came from her throat. The same appeared to be happening to the other occupants of the room, though the expressions on their faces were all totally different: elation from Nizea, astonishment from her mother, and disbelief mixed with anger from Ibrahim Khan.

"You would not joke about such a thing," he said, finding his voice at last. "So I can only conclude you mean it seriously."

"Yes, Father, I do. I mean it with all my heart. I love Fleur, and I will marry no other woman."

"Karim, don't," Fleur pleaded. "I haven't said I'll marry you. You mustn't say I . . . you've no right . . ."

Swiftly he turned upon her, keeping his voice low. "I will talk to you later. But from now on I refuse to hide what I feel." Still gripping her hand he took a few paces in his father's direction. "I won't pretend that it's been an easy decision for me. The more so since I know that your own wishes in the matter would not be the same as mine."

"At least you are honest enough to admit that," his father said angrily. "You hardly know Miss Peters. How can you stand there and talk about love?"

The muscles twitched in Karim's throat but his voice was still calm. "One doesn't need time to fall in love with a woman. One needs times to *understand* her."

"And what sort of love can there be without understanding? Surely that should come first? Only then can you say you truly love a woman enough to want her as your wife."

Karim made a disclaiming gesture with his free hand, and his father rose from his chair. "You do not realize the implication of what you are saying, my son. It will be best if we talk about it alone."

"I won't change my mind. I love Fleur."

"Does she love you?" The question was directed at her and, though she longed to deny it, she could not do so.

"Yes, I do," she said shakily. "But I haven't agreed to . . . No matter what Karim's just said, I haven't agreed to marry him. I still have to think about it."

Karim's hold momentarily loosened, and she took her chance and pulled free of him. "I haven't said yes! You know I'm speaking the truth. It isn't fair of you to rush me. I need more time."

Before he could reply to her, she ran out of the room and across the hall. She heard her name called but ignored it, knowing that if she stopped, she would be lost.

Only when she was in her bedroom with the door closed and locked behind her, did her agitation subside and anger replace it. How dare Karim put her in such an invidious position? Didn't he know that by telling his parents how he felt about her, he had made it impossible for her to stay here any longer? He might have hoped that by disclosing his feelings to them he would rush her into a decision, but instead his autocratic behavior and disregard for her feelings had only served to increase the doubts she already had about being happy with him.

Like a caged animal she paced the floor. She would return to the capital tomorrow and stay there for a couple of days. She sank into the stool before the dressing-table and stared at her reflection. Her face was flushed, her green eyes bright with tears barely held in check. She still had several weeks of vacation left, and it would give her an opportunity to fly home and talk things over with her parents. They wouldn't tell her what to do, but seeing them might help her to clarify things in her own mind. She should have done that straightaway instead of allowing Karim to bring her back here, where it was impossible for her to think clearly. When she was near him, his physical attraction was so strong that her heart overruled her head; yet when it came to her future, it was her head that she must rely on.

"Fleur, open the door!"

Karim's voice outside her door made her jump nervously to her feet. Agitatedly she backed against the wall, hoping that if she did not answer him he would go away. But it was not to be.

"Open the door," he said again. "I want to talk to you, and I don't intend to go away."

Knowing he was not the sort of man to bluff, she went across and turned the key. The door opened and she saw him in the corridor. The wall sconces were lit behind him, and his shadow loomed large across the marble floor. The black lighting gave his face an unusual harshness and turned his eyes into piercing black beams of almost laser intensity. She moved to step into the corridor, but before she could do so he strode into the room. She jumped back nervously, embarrassed by the sheets drawn back on her bed and the flimsy nightdress that lay across it.

"Wouldn't it be better if we talked downstairs?"

His glance followed hers, and a tight smile flitted over his face. "If we talk up here, you won't be able to run away from me; and you've done enough running to last us both a lifetime."

"If you don't want me to run," she said bluntly, "you shouldn't make me afraid."

"Do you always turn tail when you're afraid? I thought you were the type to stand up and fight."

"Only when I believe in what I'm fighting for."

"Don't you believe in our love?" he asked abruptly. "Are you still so fainthearted about it that you doubt me? Or do you doubt yourself? Perhaps you don't love me after all. Perhaps you were carried away by a black-haired foreigner on a white horse?"

"Don't!" she said wretchedly. "You know how I feel."

"I only know that you don't see me as an ordinary man. If you did, you wouldn't be afraid to admit that you love me."

"I'm not afraid."

"Then say it!"

"What good will it do? It still won't help me to know if I should marry you."

"At least let me hear you say it," he demanded and pulled her into his arms.

Staring into his face and feeling the warmth that emanated from him, her resistance weakened. She had put up her hands to ward him off but instead found herself placing them upon his chest. Through the thinness of his jacket, she could feel the heavy thudding of his heart; rapid beats that made her painfully conscious of his vulnerability. No longer was Karim invincible, the conqueror who had the power to destroy her, but a man of flesh and blood whose life would end if that wild heart should stop beating.

"I do love you," she gasped. "So much that I can't think logically."

"Then let *me* do the thinking. I knew I was right to tell my parents. If I had gone on waiting for you to make up your mind, I would have had to wait forever."

Fleur shivered, remembering the furious look Ibrahim Khan had flung at her. "Your father isn't happy about it. You shouldn't have told him the way you did. It was a shock to him."

"I know." He sighed heavily. "But I knew that the more time I gave you, the more unsure you'd become. I had to make the decision for you."

Another sigh escaped him, and he rested his cheek against hers. His skin was smooth and there was only the faintest trace of stubble. Involuntarily she put her hand up to it, and he caught her fingers and held them there.

"What is it?" he whispered. "Is my skin too rough for you?"

"It isn't rough at all. It's incredibly soft. Dark men usually have much stronger beards."

"At least you know I won't rasp your skin when I make love to you in the morning!" His hold on her tightened. "Now I have finally made you say you love me, when can I make you say you'll marry me?"

"I don't know. Loving you hasn't made me blind to all the reasons why our marriage won't work. You saw how your father reacted tonight; that's the way all your friends will react."

"My friends will envy me," he contradicted. "They will be furious they didn't set eyes on you first."

"Your friends might fancy me," she said with candor, "but that doesn't mean they'd want me for a wife."

"Which is a good thing because I wouldn't allow you to commit bigamy!"

"Be serious, Karim. You heard the way your father spoke at dinner. I'm sure he said what he did because he already suspected the way we felt about each other. That's why he tried to warn us."

"Warn us?" Karim was perplexed. "I don't remember him warning us about anything."

"He was talking about women giving up their careers when they got married," Fleur persisted. "He was trying to make you see that if you married someone like me, you'd have to accept different standards."

"The only standards I'm concerned with are love and loyalty and honesty and trust. Whether or not you go on working once you're my wife is immaterial to our happiness."

"But it wouldn't be. You would want me to remain at home. To put you first and my career second. You are your father's son, Karim, and . . ."

"I have my own mind," he cut in, "and I don't expect you to live the same life as my mother—or even as Nizea."

"Why shouldn't Nizea lead my sort of life?"

"Because she hasn't been brought up in the same way. You have a different cultural background."

"Then how can you believe *we'll* be happy together?"

"We love each other and our love will make the differences unimportant. But Nizea is still a child, given to dramatization. She says one thing to you, but I can assure you she believes something quite different."

"That isn't true."

"I don't want to talk about my sister. I want to talk about us—our future." His hands were warm across her back, moving over the curves of her body and pressing them close to his own. His breathing quickened and his muscles grew firm, as if he were tensing himself. "How soon will you marry me, Fleur? I can fly to England with you to meet your parents, and we can be married there."

"No!" she cried. "I need more time."

"Time will only feed your doubts. The best way to solve them is to make you mine."

His lips closed on hers, making further argument impossible. Blindly she clung to him, entranced by the broken endearments that escaped from him as he rained a storm of kisses upon her face and along the curve of her neck. Her strength left her and she clung to him, powerless to resist the onslaught of his passion. Silently he lifted her off the ground and carried her over to the bed. He placed her on it, then still keeping his arms around her, swung himself up and he rested upon her. His weight pressed her back into the softness of the coverlet and though he kept his arms firm beneath her back, she was conscious of every muscle and movement in his body. It set off a thousand answering responses in her own, awaking desires she never knew she possessed.

Until Karim had come into her life she had accepted her beauty without being aware of its power. Now she reveled in the knowledge that her beauty was causing his passion. It was foolish to be afraid. Karim loved her and wanted her happiness, seeing it as the only way of achieving his own. Of course they would have problems, but every marriage had them and, as long as there was love, the problems could be overcome.

"I need you," she whispered.

For a brief instant he resisted, then he lowered his arms, and his weight pressed her deeper into the bed. He rested upon her and she heard the swift thudding of his heart as his chest flattened her breasts. His breathing was quick, as if he had been running, and she lifted her hands to cup either side of his head. Before she could do so he swung himself off her but, as her eyes widened, he half smiled and slid over the coverlet until their bodies were again touching. His hands were deft upon her dress, making it clear why he had moved. Buttons were undone, disclosing the soft contours of her breasts, covered by a lacy brassiere. This too was undone, then the narrow belt at her waist, so that the folds of her dress slipped open.

Karim's breath caught in his throat as his eyes feasted on the creamy skin, the violet shadows between her breasts and the deeper shadow in her navel.

"Each time I see you, you grow more beautiful."

Cheeks flaming, she resorted to humor. "You see almost as much of me in a bikini."

"But in a bikini by the pool you are untouchable. Here . . ."

With infinite gentleness his fingers covered her nipples, then moved lower to let his mouth take possession. His teeth gently nibbled them, the movement arousing her to a fever pitch of desire that destroyed her embarrassment and made her cling to him. His hands curved upon her hips, the fingers delicate as feathered wing tips as he found the most intimate parts of her body, caressing, massaging, awaking sensations that lifted her to heights of undreamed of ecstasy. Yet it was ecstasy that left her wanting more, that made her curl her arms around his chest and twine her legs through his, pressing ever closer to him, as if that was the only way she could appease the aching longing within her. He writhed convulsively and, with a gasp, pushed her away from him.

"Fleur, don't! I can't take any more."

Through tangle lashes she looked at him. The muscles in his throat were visible, as if it were a physical effort to hold his need of her in check. She raised her arms towards him, and with a groan he buried his head upon her breast. His body shook as though with fever and he muttered words she could not understand. But their meaning was clear and made even clearer by the increasing intensity of his grip and the rapid thrusting of his body.

"No!" This time it was almost a shout that he gave, and he tore away from her and jumped up, keeping his back to her. His shirt was loose and with unsteady fingers he buttoned it.

"I'm sorry," she whispered. "I had no right to tempt you."

"You had every right." He swung round to look at her, backing farther away from the bed as if afraid the sight of her would tempt him again. "It was only your innocence that protected you. You still don't realize how potent you are."

"Only because I'm not used to you."

"I'll never get used to *you*," he said drily. "The more I have of you, the more I'll want." Fire glinted in his eyes. "Does the prospect frighten you?"

"I'm only frightened that my innocence might . . ." Remembering the last half hour, she frowned. "There's so much I don't know."

"I wouldn't worry about it." The words were spoken quietly. "For an amateur you did better than well. A couple more hours in my arms, and you'll be giving lessons to *me!*"

Her laugh was tremulous, and she loved him deeply for his sympathetic understanding of her fears.

"You have nothing to worry about, my heart." He was close beside her again, bending low to gaze into her eyes. "Don't you know what it does to me to feel you beneath me? Your softness and warmth; the way your breasts swell and grow hard and the roundness of your belly which is so soft." He lowered his head and pressed his lips to the corner of her mouth. "Go on blushing, my flower of the desert. You don't realize the power you have over me, nor do you realize that I will love you until the end of my days."

"Oh, Karim, I love you too. But I can't say it in such wonderful words."

"Actions speak louder than words," he reminded her and drew her hand on to his body. For a moment he held it there, then with a sigh he let it go.

"Comb your hair, and we will go downstairs and see my parents. They are expecting us."

Panic brought her to a sitting position. "Can't we leave it until tomorrow?"

"And have you spend a sleepless night worrying what my father will say? No, dearest, we will go down now."

His look brooked no argument and she smoothed her dress, ran a comb quickly through her hair, then followed him out, deeply afraid yet drawing comfort from the warmth of the fingers entwined with hers.

Eleven

TO *Fleur's surprise, Ibrahim Khan* received her as his prospective daughter-in-law with far more conviviality than she had expected. He even suggested that they give a party to introduce her to all their family and friends, an offer with delighted Karim, who couldn't understand Fleur's dismay at the prospect.

"I still want time to get to know *you,*" she explained. "I can always meet your relations later."

"Later—later. What's wrong with the word 'sooner'?" He was half angry, half joking. "Don't you know how impatient I am to make you mine?"

"Of course, I know. But I don't feel as if we've had any courtship."

It was the best thing she could have said, for he was instantly contrite.

"Now I feel I've cheated you out of something wonderful. But I was so afraid of losing you that I didn't have time to woo you slowly, the way you would have liked."

She smiled. "I can see I'll have to get used to an impatient lover."

"Never impatient as a lover," he said against her mouth. "No matter how great my need for you, I will always wait until you are ready for me." His tongue snaked along her lips, lightly penetrated her mouth, and then withdrew. "Though the last few times I've held you in my arms doesn't make me feel I will have to wait long!"

She buried her head against his shoulder. "I hope I'll be able to satisfy you."

"Never." He deliberately misunderstood her. "I'll always be hungry for you. That's a feeling I must learn to live with." He tilted her chin until he could gaze into her eyes. "From now on I will give you a courtship to remember."

"It isn't necessary," she protested, but knew from the look on his face that she might as well save her breath.

During the next month, Karim was the personification of an ardent suitor, returning twice a week to spend the night at the villa, and telephoning her on the nights when he was away. Each weekend he arrived with lavish gifts for her, not one or two, but half a dozen, sometimes even more, until finally she was forced to protest that this was not courtship but outright spoiling.

"You won't know what spoiling means until we are married," he said.

"I thought that's when the spoiling stopped!"

"Not for us." His look was a caress and she marveled that this quick-witted, masterful man should have chosen her to be his wife from among all the other beautiful and intelligent women he knew.

"But none are as intelligent and beautiful as you," he said later that Friday evening, when she mentioned it to him. "How much longer are you going to keep me waiting before you set a date for our wedding?"

"I've been thinking about it," she said. "Would Christmas be all right?"

The look on his face told her it wouldn't, and she added defensively: "I can't walk out on Madame Nadar. My contract with her doesn't end until next April. But if I explained why I wanted to leave earlier . . ."

"I won't wait until Christmas." Karim's voice held a silkiness she had come to expect when he was holding his temper in check. Had he ranted and raved, it would have been less frightening, for quietness meant he was also in control of himself. "You will write to Madame Nadar and ask her to release you at once. At the latest I wish to marry you in October."

"I can't walk out on the school. They'll need to find another teacher to replace me."

"There's no shortage of teachers in Teheran."

"There's a shortage of *English* teachers." It was an effort not to snap but she was anxious to be as cool as he was. "You said you'd give me time, Karim, and now you're going back on your word."

"No, I'm not." His voice was silkier than ever. "I have given you plenty of time, Fleur, and now I'm becoming impatient."

They were sitting together in the garden, and he slid along the seat until his leg was touching hers. The hardness of his thigh set her blood racing.

"Is it so hard for you to understand why I'm anxious to make you my wife? This life we're leading is unnatural. To have to say goodnight to you each evening . . . you don't know what it does to me."

"Yes, I do," she admitted. "It does the same to me."

"Then why make us wait? Marry me soon, my heart."

His gentleness was her undoing, as it always was, and she nodded. "I'll write to Madame Nadar tomorrow and ask her to find a replacement as soon as she can."

"And then we'll fly to England to meet your parents," Karim whispered against her mouth.

As her arms came up around his neck, she heard footsteps and drew back. Ibrahim Khan came into view, his cream-colored tropical suit gleaming pale in the moonlight.

"Do you want me, Father?" Karim asked, rising.

"There is a call for you from Paris. It is Monsieur Legrand."

Touching Fleur lightly on the shoulder, Karim strode off.

Fleur wished she could follow him but knew it would be rude. She remained where she was, stiffening slightly as Ibrahim Khan settled beside her.

"I am sorry to interrupt your tête-à-tête," he said.

"It doesn't matter. We were only talking about—about setting a date for our wedding."

"Only?" He paused. "I have the impression you are reluctant to do so."

"Engagements are fun." She tried to keep her voice light. "But Karim is impatient for us to be married."

"My son has always been impatient when he has

wanted something. Occasionally he has regretted that impatience."

The implication was obvious, and she took up the challenge, faintly surprised that he should have made it.

"Are you saying you think he will regret marrying me?"

"I think it is quite possible."

"I'm sorry you do," Fleur said shakily. "I suppose it's because you . . . because you disapprove of me?"

"I do not disapprove of you, my child, only of your suitability as a wife for my son. You are too intelligent for me to enumerate my reasons."

"Yes," she sighed. "I know them all."

"Yet you deny their truth?"

"I deny their truth as applied to Karim and myself. We love each other enough to work things out."

"That is the age-old cry of lovers," came the answer. "But you will find that your marriage will be no different from anyone else's. In a year, maybe a little longer, you will find your differences growing, not lessening."

"Why do you say that?"

"Because I know my son. For the moment he is willing to give you your own way in everything. His passion for you is making him weak. But once his passion has been satiated, his strength will return, and with it will come his desire to be master in his own house."

"It will be my house, too," Fleur said quickly. "Marriage is a partnership."

"If by that you mean that a husband and wife each have their own duties to perform then I agree with you. But you must make sure you know what those duties are. Yours will be to take care of your home; to bear your husband's children, and to put your heart into everything that is of interest to him. His duty will be to provide for you and his family and to treat you with honor and respect. But there will never be any question as to whose word is law."

Fleur was silent. To say she did not believe Karim thought this way would only lead to an argument.

"I know you don't believe me," the older man went on. "Even if you asked Karim, he would deny the truth of what I'm saying."

"He wouldn't lie," Fleur said sharply.

"Of course not." Ibrahim Khan looked affronted at the very idea. "My son would believe he is saying the truth, because at the moment he thinks he is. But once you are married he will find it impossible not to follow the traditions he has been taught."

Again Fleur held her tongue.

"I am sorry you still disagree with me," the man went on. "For I am your friend and wish only your happiness. You won't find that with my son. Of that I am sure."

Fleur tried to hold herself away from the words but they absorbed her, weighing her down with their import. How wily was the man who sat beside her. He knew full well that to rage at her would have given her the strength to refute what he was saying. Instead he had approached her with guile and subtly planted his seeds of doubt.

"If you are so much against our marriage, Mr. Khan, why did you offer to give a big party for us?"

"Because to argue with my son would encourage him in his obstinacy."

"But if you don't argue, then he'll marry me."

"I know. But he will also retain his respect for me and

will not be ashamed to come and tell me when . . ."
Ibrahim Khan rose. "Shall we walk to the pool?"

She rose and bravely finished his sentence. "Even before I marry your son, you're looking ahead to the divorce."

"I am a realist. I do not think it would be kind of me to lie to you."

"Even a realist can be wrong!"

"Perhaps. If you love my son enough and are willing to give in to him and be the wife he wants, then your marriage may well satisfy him."

Fleur was repelled by the word "satisfied." It seemed to turn her into a chattel. But that was the way Ibrahim Khan regarded women. Even his wife, despite her luxurious life, had to ask her husband for everything she wanted and would not dare cross him in any way. But things would be different between herself and Karim, no matter what his father said to the contrary.

With relief she saw Karim approaching, his long legs diminishing the distance between them until he was by her side, his warm hands finding her cold, trembling ones. Instinctively, he knew she was upset, and the way he stroked her fingers reassured her.

"I think I've managed to explain to Monsieur Legrand why I changed one of the clauses in the contract," Karim addressed his father. "But I'll send him a resumé of our telephone conversation, and if he has any other queries, he can tell me."

"He is a nervous man," Mr. Khan said. "He knows your reputation as a lawyer and thinks you're trying to get the better of him."

"I know," Karim said wryly. "When I saw him a few

months ago, I happened to mention I'd worked in London for a year with Benson & Bates."

"You must be first-rate," Fleur commented. "I don't know many law firms but even *I* have heard of them."

"They wanted my son to remain with them as a partner," Ibrahim Khan said proudly.

"Why didn't you?" Fleur asked.

"I preferred to be a big fish in a little pond," Karim smiled.

"And now you are a big fish in a big pond," his father added.

"I regret that, too. If I had my time again, I'd keep my practice small and maybe have only one or two big clients."

"You are being foolish. You have worked like a Trojan to reach your present position. You are internationally known, and you are your own master. If you were a small-time lawyer you would be at the beck and call of others."

"Not all men set great store on being their own masters," Fleur intervened.

"You are talking of unambitious men," Ibrahim Khan dismissed her statement. "And it is foolish of you to encourage my son in his childish talk."

Fleur gave Karim a beseeching look, but he ignored it. There was a brooding expression on his face that she would have given much to be able to decipher.

"Let's go for a walk, Fleur," he said quietly, and at the same time put his hand on his father's arm in a gesture which she saw as placatory.

"Do you think your father's right?" she asked the moment they were out of earshot. "Is that why you didn't defend me?"

"I didn't think you needed defending. You have always stood up very well for yourself in any discussion."

"But do you agree with what your father said?" she persisted. "That I'd be wrong to encourage you to be less ambitious?"

"The question is irrelevant. I have a big law firm and am well established in it."

"But you said you wished you had a smaller company."

"I was talking for the sake of talking," Karim shrugged. "My father realized that."

"And I didn't," Fleur said flatly. "Which means he knows you better than I do."

"Temporarily. Soon *you* will know me better than anyone."

She did not respond to this, and her lack of expression made him stop walking so that he could study her carefully.

"What did my father say to you when you were alone together?"

"Nothing."

"You aren't telling me the truth. But I will allow you to keep your secret. Women like to have one. They feel it gives them strength."

"I'll need strength against you," she murmured. "Otherwise you'll try to dominate me."

"And be your master," he teased. "That's what you're afraid of. Yet I have no objection to you being my mistress!"

Despite her unease, she couldn't help smiling and was glad when Karim saw it as a sign of her contentment and took her into his arms. Close to him her doubts were always appeased, and she could think of the future without fear; it was only when they were apart that her anxiety arose. Perhaps it would be better if they were married quickly.

With this in mind Fleur wrote to Madame Nadar the following morning and, since Karim was returning to Teheran after lunch, he suggested taking the letter with him and having his chauffeur deliver it. He did not ask what she had said in it, though the warmth in her eyes as she looked at him must have given him some clue, for his own eyes darkened with passion, the fire in them telling her all that his lips could not utter.

As always, Karim's departure left her depressed, and she used work as a palliative, a fact which Nizea noted with grumbling amusement. Of all the Khans she was the one whom Fleur knew to be genuinely delighted by her engagement, and they spent happy hours talking of the future. Nizea saw Fleur's entry into the family as the first opening of a wedge that would eventually lead to her own freedom.

"Once you're Karim's wife, you'll be able to persuade my father to let me go to the university."

"I wouldn't bank on it. I've already spoken to Karim, and he says he won't interfere."

"It will be different when you're married. You will have more influence over him then."

Fleur recollected Ibrahim Khan's comment. "I might have less."

"Don't be silly. Once you belong to Karim, he'll dote on you."

"I won't belong to your brother," Fleur said sharply,

"any more than he'll belong to me. Marriage is a partnership, and I wouldn't dream of forcing him to do something against his will. Nor would I use his need of me to get my own way."

"I bet he'll use your love for *him* to get what he wants," Nizea said. "Karim's as subtle as a serpent."

Fleur was disquieted at the picture of marriage as portrayed by Nizea. This was not the way she envisaged her relationship with Karim, and she wondered how many other unknown facets there were in his character. The question lay below the surface of her mind, giving her unpleasant dreams at night and marring the tranquility of the long sunny days.

Halfway through the week she received a call from Rory. She had not written to tell him of her engagement, reluctant to do so until her parents knew, which wouldn't be until she and Karim flew to England. Because she knew Rory considered her to be free, she assumed he was ringing to ask when she was returning to Teheran and was taken aback to hear him say he was flying up the following day to Babol—one of the more important towns on the Caspian coast—and hoped she would be free to meet him for lunch.

"I'm going to England at the weekend," he explained. "For good, this time."

Swallowing this second surprise, she said: "Isn't it rather sudden? I thought you were going to be here for another year."

"That was the original intention, but I've been offered a junior partnership with Benson & Bates."

The name rang a bell in her mind, and she remembered Karim telling her he had once worked for the company.

"They're an excellent firm," Rory continued. "And it's too good an offer for me to turn down. Do say you can meet me," he pleaded. "I'd hate like hell to go back without having another chance to propose."

"I'll only see you on condition that you don't," she said firmly. "I mean it, Rory."

There was a short pause.

"I take the point, Fleur. Let's just meet for old time's sake."

Wishing she could avoid it, for she was sure nothing would stop him from repeating his proposal, she agreed to meet him in Babol at noon the next day.

"Let's have an early lunch," she suggested, knowing Karin always returned late in the afternoon for the Friday and Saturday weekend.

"The earlier the better," Rory said. "Then I'll get to spend more time with you."

This was not what Fleur had in mind, but she did not argue and replaced the receiver to see Nizea looking at her curiously.

"That was Rory." Fleur felt it incumbent on her to explain. "He's coming to Babol on business, and I'm having lunch with him."

"Try and get to Babolsar at the same time. It's a bit further along the coast and has a wonderful palace. In fact, if you went straight to the palace you could arrange to meet your friend there instead of in Babol. There's a fine restaurant close by that serves the best caviar in the world."

"It would be wasted on me," Fleur said. "I think it's like highly salted cod's roe."

"You're an infidel," Nizea giggled.

"I know. But Rory isn't, so I'll take your advice and call him back. I'm sure he won't mind a drive along the coast if there's a good tuck-in at the end of it."

The next day, watching Rory gustily tackling a mound of glistening black caviar smothered in sour cream, she was glad she had taken Nizea's advice.

"At least you'll remember this lunch for a long time to come," she smiled at him.

"I'll remember *you* even longer. I hate the thought of going back to England and leaving you behind."

"It's better for you to forget me," she said hastily. "Then you'll have more chance of meeting someone else."

"Do you think one can fall in and out of love on command?"

"I think you're too sensible to waste time pining for a girl who doesn't want you," she said firmly and, looking at his freckled face and amiable smile, knew how unlike Karim he was. Of course, Rory would be easier to live with and, though one might never attain the heights with him, neither would one reach the lows that life with Karim might bring. Apart from any difficulties, there was the social aspect too. Although plenty of English people lived in the capital, as the wife of a Persian she would be regarded as the next best thing to a foreigner.

The urge to tell Rory all that was going through her mind was overwhelming, and she was only forestalled by his suddenly seeing some business friends on the other side of the room and beckoning them to join him for coffee. By the time they left the restaurant her urge to confide had evaporated, and she was in control of herself.

"Now for some sight-seeing," he said. "We can't come all the way here without looking at the palace."

It would have been churlish to refuse, and Fleur gave in with grace, finding that, against her will, the beauty of the restored building made her lose all sense of time. She was later leaving Rory than she had intended, for he had insisted on her sending the Khans' car and chauffeur home, saying he would drive her back instead.

It was well after five when he drew up outside the gates of the villa whose white walls could only be glimpsed through the barrier of trees.

"I assume it's awkward for you to ask me in," he said drily.

"Why should it be?" She kept her voice calm, knowing that the moment he entered the house he would learn of her engagement to Karim. She should have told him during lunch, when she had first wanted to do it.

"It's too late for me to call your bluff," he grinned. "I have to get back to Babol for an evening meeting." He caught hold of her hands, which were resting in her lap. "You will write to me, won't you?"

"No," she said firmly. "When I come to London, I'll give you a call."

"You're a very hard-headed girl."

"And you're a very obstinate man."

"Will you give me a good-bye kiss?"

She held up her face, and he caught her in a bearlike hug and kissed her full on the mouth, letting his lips linger there before drawing away. "I always knew you were too beautiful for me," he said, his eyes extra bright. "God, how I envy the man who finally gets you."

He reached for her again, but she eluded his grip and slipped from the car. She tried to speak but was afraid she would cry; so she just stood there and waved good-bye to him. When Rory left Iran, she would be totally alone in this alien country. It was a frightening thought. She told herself she was ridiculous to feel this way, for she would be with the man who was going to be her husband; but somehow she was not reassured.

She hurried through the garden and was walking along the cloistered terrace with its beautifully tiled walls and floor, when Karim appeared from behind one of the pillars. His formal clothes, a silk suit in dark blue, told her he had not long arrived from Teheran, and she was put out that she had not managed to get back even a few minutes ahead of him. Irritation rose in her that she should feel this way. Karim was not her jailer. He was the man she loved, and she was not afraid of him. Wishing to prove it, she ran towards him, hands outstretched.

He made no answering gesture of welcome, and his arms remained motionless at his side, though his hands were clenching and unclenching. She came to a stop a couple of feet away from him, trying not to show she was disturbed by his aloofness.

"Have you been back long, Karim? I went out to lunch and hoped to get back earlier."

"No doubt you did—then I needn't have known."

"It wasn't a secret."

"Evidently." Though low, his voice was harsh. "You don't care how much you shame me as long as you do what you want."

"Shame you? How can my going out with Rory shame you?"

"You dare ask that?"

He reached out as if to get hold of her, and she backed away, frightened by the raw fury on his face. Part of her was thrilled by his jealousy, but another part of her was disgusted, seeing his attitude as an insult to her integrity.

"You're making a fuss over nothing, Karim. Rory is going back to England and, as he was coming up to Babol, he asked if he could see me."

"If he had wanted you to go to Teheran, would you have gone there, too?"

"Probably. What's so terrible about it? He's a friend of mine."

"He's in love with you."

"What's that got to do with it?"

"Everything! You had no business to see him. You're mine. Mine, do you hear? You should know better than to meet a man who desires you."

"Am I allowed to meet only men who don't?" She forced herself to give a cool laugh. "Honestly, Karim, you're talking like a fool."

"How dare you call me a fool?" This time his hand shot out and caught her by the arm, his grip so tight that the pain numbed her. "Do you think my love for you is such a weakness that you can do what you like with me? Well, I'll show you otherwise."

His head came down swiftly, and his mouth fastened on hers in a kiss of such demanding ferocity that she felt the salt taste of blood on her tongue. There was too much pain in his touch for it to arouse desire, and she tried to pull away from him. Her resistance increased his fury and he intensified the pressure of his mouth. Her breath was stifled, and she beat her palms against his back.

"You're mine," he said thickly. "I won't have you giving your beauty to anyone else."

"I'm not your slave," she panted and again tried to pull herself free of him.

"Be still," he ordered and dragged her hard up against his chest.

She knew it was impossible to escape him and that to try would only increase his anger. Yet it required all her will power to remain motionless and silent, for inside she was seething with anger. How dare he talk to her as if she were his slave? Did he think she had no mind of her own that he could tell her what to do and expect her to obey him unthinkingly?

"I cannot bear other men to see you," he ground out, winding his fingers around the strands of her hair.

The feel of its silkiness seemed to affect him, for he began to tremble. Sensing it, her anger died like a flame in water, replaced by the aching knowledge that she could not judge Karim the way she would judge any other man she knew. No longer was he the sophisticated man of education she had agreed to marry but a primitive tyrant whose cruel demands were but an echo of his ancestors.

"I can't bear any other man to have your smile," he muttered against her lips. "You belong to me and no one else."

His hands moved down her slender back, pressing her hard against him so that it was impossible not to feel the desire she aroused in him. In normal circumstances she would have been thrilled by it, but now she was sickened. All he was concerned with were his own needs. To him she was a body he wanted to take. She was not allowed to have a mind, and any resistance she offered would be crushed until he had turned her into a shrinking, submissive creature who would obey his every whim. Limply she leaned against him, but her thoughts raced on, and a bitterness she had never suspected within herself directed its corrosiveness toward him.

For endless moments Karim satiated himself with her body. His lips moved from her mouth to the white throat, rested on the shadow between her breasts and nibbled along the smooth line of her shoulder to the nape of her neck and the curve of her ear.

"I love you," he groaned. "I can't bear to be away from you. I want you with me wherever I go. *Darling . . . darling . . .*"

At last he released her, slowly withdrawing his hands and stepping away from her. He was in perfect control of himself again. His features had lost their harshness, and his mouth was a delicate curve, the full, lower lip once more held in. His eyes had lost their dramatic glitter and were almost tender as they rested on her.

"Forgive me if I have hurt you, my dearest. I hope that from now on you won't try to make me jealous."

Casually she walked several paces away from him until she reached a chair. She didn't sit in it but went behind it, as if in need of its protection.

"I didn't try to make you jealous, Karim. I agreed to have lunch with Rory, because it never entered my head that you would object."

"I don't object to you having lunch with a friend, but this man wishes to be more than that."

"He's still my friend, and he's accepted the fact that I won't marry him."

"Is that why he kissed you on the mouth when he said good-bye?"

Fleur was glad she was a long way from Karim for she saw the fury rising again in him.

"Were you spying on me?" she flared.

"I was walking in the garden and waiting for you. I heard the car draw up at the gate and was coming to greet you when I witnessed the loving farewell."

"It was a farewell between friends."

"Is that all he was to you? Are you sure he wasn't your lover?"

Staggered by the accusation, she stared at him blankly.

"Well," he demanded, "aren't you going to deny it?"

"Would you believe me if I did? You may enjoy torturing yourself, Karim, but I'm not going to let you torture *me*."

"Answer me!" he cried, as if he had not heard her. "I demand to know the truth."

"About Rory?" Her voice was icy as her eyes. "Of course, he was my lover. That's why I followed him out here. And he wasn't the first man, either. There have been dozens and dozens! Each one better than the last!"

"Be quiet!" Karim almost shouted the words. "You're lying to me. You're innocent. I've seen it on your face . . . felt it in your touch." He put a shaking hand to his forehead. "I shouldn't have spoken to you the way I did. I must have been mad. But you make me so angry that . . ."

"I make *you* angry?" Her voice rose high, and she made no attempt to lower it, not caring that it rang out in the soft evening air. "It's about time you stopped thinking of yourself and consider how *I* feel. I'm not one of your servant girls that you can order around. I've taken care of myself for years, and no one has ever dictated to me."

"I wasn't dictating."

"How else would you describe it? As bullying? As domineering? As proving you were my lord and master? Well, you're not, and you never will be. Never!"

She flung the chair forward, and it slithered across the tiles. He tried to side-step it and come to her but, before he could do so, she ran across the hall and up the stairs as if the devil was at her heels—as indeed she felt he was—except that the devil was named Karim, the man she loved and feared.

Only when she was in the safety of her room, with the door locked and the balcony window bolted, did her heart steady its wild beating. What sort of future would she have with a man who could turn from angel to devil in a matter of seconds? It was hopeless to think of it. They didn't see love in the same way. To her it meant trust, understanding, tenderness. To him it meant control, mastering, and the total domination of her will power.

She sank trembling on to the bed and lowered her flushed face into her hands. She and Karim were too different ever to come to terms with each other. The love which she had thought might bring them together had instead driven them irretrievably apart.

Twelve

LOATH *though she was to arouse Ibrahim Khan's suspicion that things were not well between herself and his son, Fleur found it impossible to go down to dinner that night. The thought of food nauseated her and the prospect of sitting at the onyx table making banal conversation, or having to listen in respectful silence while the two men discussed business affairs, was more than she could tolerate. How unlike her own family's dinnertime conversation, when everyone was allowed to chip in and say what they liked from the youngest member to the eldest.

I must have been crazy to think of marrying him, she decided. *He doesn't want a woman, he wants a dummy.* She knew she was having to stoke her anger against him to keep it going full blast; if she didn't, she would remember him in other moods, and the memory would reawaken her love for him.

She pulled at the tasseled wall bell and a moment later heard the shuffle of steps outside her door. Swiftly she unlocked it and asked the servant girl to tell Madame Khan she was remaining in her room for the rest of the evening. Then she relocked the door and went into the bathroom to shower. The warm water soothed her bruised lips, though it could not wash away the actual bruises that Karim's fingers had made on top of her arms, and she was conscious of them as she dried herself and slipped into a primrose nightdress. It was short and full skirted and, with a slip underneath, could easily have been worn during the day. She picked up a brush and ran it through her hair. At last the tension was leaving her, and she felt unexpectedly tired, worn out by the emotion of Karim's fury.

Kicking off her mules, she went over to the bed. She plumped the pillows high and then slipped between the sheets. She would read and relax and try not to think of the future until tomorrow. But the present would not let itself be denied as she thought of the family sitting in the dining room and wondered if Mr. or Mrs. Khan or Nizea had commented on her absence and what Karim had said about it—if anything.

From the garden below her window came soft night sounds, and she pushed aside one of the silk sheets covering her and allowed the cool air to blow upon her skin. There was a gentle knock at the door. Her mouth went dry and before she could ask who it was, the soft voice of a servant told her she had brought her some food.

Fleur slipped across to unlock the door and then returned to bed. The tray was placed on her lap. It had four small legs and served as a table, keeping the weight of the dishes away from her. In hesitant English the maid asked if there was anything else she required, and Fleur, after a quick glance at the dishes set before her, shook her head. The bowls of savory rice were not as acceptable as a bacon sandwich would have been at this precise moment, but it was a great deal better than nothing, and she tackled them hungrily, surprised she should have regained her appetite.

Now she was able to think more logically of her scene with Karim, though this did not diminish her fears for the future. A big question mark still hung over her, and she wished there was someone to whom she could turn for advice. Yet in the end it all rested on her love for Karim and whether or not it was strong enough to enable her way of life to fit in with his. For the first time she saw how foreign his way would be and had severe doubts about her ability to come to terms with it. Even if she did, how long would this willingness remain, and wasn't there the risk that one day she would begin to find it unacceptable?

That was exactly what Ibrahim Khan had said. What a wily old bird he was! He had made few critical comments to her since Karim's disclosure that he wished to marry her, but those few had been telling ones and—as she did now—she found herself remembering them. Was it true that once Karim had made her his wife his love for her would diminish and, with it, his tolerance of their differences? Did this mean his jealousy would decrease? Or would it increase because he would then see her as someone over whom he had control?

The arrival of the maid with some coffee was a welcome interruption and, when she was alone again, she resolutely tried to put Karim from her mind. Night was never a good time to try to work out a solution to one's problems; it heightened one's sensitivity and made one react like an overcharged battery. But would she be any nearer a solution in the brightness of the day?

Again her thoughts were interrupted by a knock at the door. Her heart thudded in her throat, and she was not surprised to hear Karim's voice asking if he could enter.

At her call, he did so, and stood looking at her across the width of the room. Even from this distance she noticed the pallor of his skin. It made his eyes look unnaturally dark and the lids heavier.

"Are you feeling better?" he asked.

"I wasn't ill." She heard how steady her voice sounded and wondered if Karim's calm question had hidden the same amount of emotion.

"I assumed you weren't feeling well," he said, "because you didn't come down to dinner."

"I was too angry to see you," she said bluntly.

"I thought so. I have come up to apologize."

He came across the floor and paused at the foot of the bed. He had changed from his dark suit to a pale-colored one, and his shirt was creamy and frilled down the front. He looked incredibly handsome and, had he been her husband at this moment, she would have flung herself into his arms and begged him to stay. The thought of such weakness frightened her, for she knew that passion was not the solution to the problems between them. As Ibrahim Khan had said, when passion went, there had to be something else to take its place; and she was not sure whether there was anything else between herself and Karim.

"Will you forgive me, Fleur?" he said again.

"I can't forget the fact that you see me as your possession."

"I see you as the woman I love."

"But that turns me into your possession."

"Don't you do the same with me?" He gripped the foot of the bed. "Weren't you jealous when you saw me with Ferada? I saw the way you kept watching me and the anger in your eyes."

"There's a difference between normal jealousy and obsessiveness!"

The breath caught in his throat. "Is that how you see my love for you?"

"Yes," she said curtly. "And I hate it!"

He came round to the side of the bed. His eyes moved over her face as if he were trying to guess what was going on in her mind. Suddenly he leaned forward and caught hold of her. She winced at the pressure of his hands and instantly his eyes went to the bruises on her flesh. Slowly the blood seeped into his cheeks.

"Did I—did I do that?"

"My lover didn't," she said bitterly, "so it must have been the man who *professes* to love me!"

With a stifled cry he knelt beside her. His head was on a level with her breasts, and the bedside lamp played on the darkness of his hair. Aware of his physical nearness and the way it aroused her, she steeled herself against responding to it.

"Words aren't enough to tell you how much I hate myself," he whispered. "If I could take your pain, I would do so willingly."

"I would rather you understood me," she said huskily. "It's the only way you will be able to control your jealousy."

"When you're my wife, it will be better. Then I won't have any doubts."

"If you doubt me now, you will always doubt me. Putting a ring on my finger won't make you trust me more."

"As my wife you will be too busy to go out with other men." His eyes gleamed. "You will have children to take care of and a demanding man to satisfy."

Her senses were stirred by his words, but with it also came a revulsion from them, and she drew back against the pillows.

"I hate it when you say things like that. Making love to you and having your children won't stop me from wanting to have friends and a life of my own. I won't just sit at home like an empty vessel, waiting for you to come back to fill it. I'm not a pet, Karim, I'm a human being."

"I know." He reached for her hand and twined his fingers through hers. "I'm human too, my darling. That's why I can't remain here with you." His eyes glowed as they moved over her, resting on the skin that gleamed through the primrose chiffon, and the curves of her body that were molded by the silken sheet that lay upon her. "I suggest we leave any further discussion until tomorrow."

"Very well."

He straightened, half put out his hand again, then turned and strode out. Fleur leaned against the pillows dejectedly. Karim had not accepted one word she had said. He believed her to be overtired and was still treating her as if she didn't know her own mind. He thought everything could be solved by his lovemaking and, though this might be true for the first few years of their life together, it was no foundation on which to build a marriage.

Next morning she was downstairs before any other members of the household. Only the servants moved silently through the rooms, their long robes turning them into shameless blue bundles. The faces of the women were half hidden, and only their eyes were visible. It was the sight of these women that reminded her of the life and culture of the man she loved. She tried to picture him in England, among her own family and friends, and speculated how he would react to them. There was much about him that would never change, yet surely the cooler temperaments with which he would be surrounded would rub off on him?

She was deep in thought and sipping her second coffee of the day when Mrs. Khan joined her. Only rarely did the woman put in an appearance before lunchtime, usually spending the morning in her own quarters.

"My husband and I are going to lunch with friends," she said, settling herself in a basket chair on the terrace. "We hoped you and Karim would come with us, but he said last night that he wanted to spend the day alone with you."

Fleur was annoyed that he had made the decision without asking her whether she wanted to go, though she would probably have said the same.

"Do your friends live nearby?"

"About fifty kilometers away. They have recently built a beautiful villa, and my husband is anxious to see it. If he likes it, he thought of using the same architect to design your summer home."

Fleur looked up from her coffee. "I'm not sure I want one. If we live in the northern part of Teheran, there doesn't seem much point in having a summer place. Anyway, with air conditioning there isn't the same need to rush out of the city."

"Karim relaxes more when he is away from Teheran," Mrs. Khan chided gently. "Surely you want what is best for him?"

"I think Karim and I should decide together what we want," Fleur said, equally gently. "I don't believe in one partner making the decision for the other. It should be mutual."

"We don't see it in the same way. We believe a wife and a husband each brings something different to a marriage."

"I know," Fleur said bitterly. "The wife gives and the husband takes!"

"But the wife is always glad to give. It makes her feel needed."

"You mean she enjoys subjugating herself?" Fleur set her coffee cup down sharply. "Well, I wouldn't. Nor would I want my husband to expect me to do it."

"You have very strong ideas about what you want your husband to do," Mrs. Khan said. "You might find life less difficult if you were more pliant. Don't fight Karim, my dear." The dark eyes, far softer than her husband's, surveyed Fleur with gentle reproach. "I know you are too thoughtful to quarrel with him in the presence of myself and my husband, but we are aware of the tension that exists between you. You seem to want to resist Karim and, of course, that makes him more determined to dominate you. If you would give in to him a little . . . Women should pretend, you know. We can gain far more that way."

"But I'm afraid . . . it isn't *my* way. I wasn't brought up to pretend—even if it's the best way of getting what I want. I have no intention of allowing Karim to dominate me."

"He can't help it; it's his nature. Would you clip the wings of an eagle?"

"I don't see how the simile applies."

"But it does. Karim is only happy when he is in control. In his professional and personal life he has to be the one in charge." The dark head, untouched by gray, tilted to one side as the older woman surveyed the younger. "Look at me, Fleur. Am I not a happy and fulfilled woman? And that is exactly what I want for you."

"But I'm not like you," Fleur protested. "I wouldn't be happy with the things that make you happy."

"Then how do you expect to be happy with Karim when he is exactly like his father?"

The words hit Fleur with the impact of a sledge hammer. To see Karim as the son of his father was difficult enough; to see Karim as a replica was more than she had bargained for.

"He . . . he isn't," she stammered. "He's had a different education. He's lived in England and America and . . ."

"He is a Khan," came the quiet reply. "Now that he is back in his own country—among his own people—what he did when he was abroad counts for nothing. If you wish to spend your life with him, this country and its people must become yours."

The words were an echo of those that Ruth had said to Naomi, her mother-in-law, but Fleur knew she would never be able to utter them. This country and its people would always be alien to her. It was something she was only now beginning to comprehend, and the implication of what it meant had to be carefully considered.

Footsteps resounded on the marble floor, and Karim spoke from the hall. "I hope I'm not interrupting anything."

"I was telling Fleur you wish to spend the day alone with her. I think she is disappointed not to be seeing the villa."

"We can drive over one afternoon," he said easily. "Omar has given me permission to look at it any time I like."

"You have everything worked out," his mother said fondly and smiled at Fleur as she rose, as if to show that this only served to indicate the truth of what she had said a little earlier.

It was not until his mother had left them that Karim perched on a chair, swinging one long leg immaculately clad in beige cord slacks. "You are still looking pale, my heart. That's why I thought it best if we didn't go on a long journey today."

"Fifty kilometers isn't far. You should at least have asked me."

"Don't you want us to spend the day by ourselves? Nizea is going with my parents, and we will be alone in the house."

"With ten servants."

He snapped his fingers to indicate they were nothing, and she gave an irritated shrug. She was glad he wished to be alone with her and knew it was churlish not to admit it. Yet the highhanded way he had made the decision prevented her.

"How remiss of me!" he said suddenly and, reaching into the pocket of his shirt, took out an envelope. "I meant to give you this yesterday but in the heat of our—er—discussion, I forgot."

She took the envelope and recognized Madame Nadar's handwriting.

"She sent it to my office by a servant," he explained. "You know how unreliable the post is. A letter is delivered here more quickly from New York than from one side of Teheran to the other."

She smiled and, slitting open the envelope, extracted the letter. It expressed delight at her engagement and was gushing with best wishes for her happiness.

"You must not think of continuing to teach here. I know how eager you are to be with your fiancé, and I have immediately contacted the agency in London with whom I was dealing before I engaged you. I am quite sure they won't have any trouble in sending me another English teacher at once. She may not have all your excellent qualifications but please have no misgivings at leaving me. I am more than delighted to do everything I can to insure the happiness of any member of the Khan family."

Anger such as she had not known filled Fleur. Silently she folded the letter and replaced it in its envelope. Her hands were shaking—as was her whole body—and she refused to look in Karim's direction.

"Well," he said complacently, "aren't you pleased?"

"You know the contents," she stated without surprise.

"Naturally. She telephoned me before she sent the letter round."

"To make sure it met with your approval?"

"What's this?" he said in perplexity. "You surely can't be angry because she's released you? Don't you know what it means? We needn't wait until October." He came to stand close to her. "We can fly to England next week to see your parents, and then we can arrange our marraige."

"No!" she cried sharply. "We can't. I won't do it! You had no right to ask Madame Nadar to release me. I made it clear when I spoke to you that I wanted to stay with her until October."

"Only because you felt it to be your duty. You said it would take her time to replace you, and all I did was to ask her to expedite it."

"You mean you ordered her to do it," Fleur snapped. "Why couldn't you leave things alone? Who gave you the right to interfere?"

"What's this talk of right?" he demanded, flinging his hands wide. "I want your happiness, and you want mine. That's the only criterion that counts."

"No, Karim, it isn't. People have to be left to make their own decisions about what's right for them; and I had already made mine. I told Madame I wanted to remain at the school until October. Even then you knew I felt guilty at letting her down."

"You haven't let her down," he said impatiently. "She's just told you she's getting a replacement."

"She's doing what you asked her to do. And you had no business to interfere."

"I refuse to discuss it further." Karim was suddenly angry. "You are behaving like a child. All I did was make things easier for you—for us—and you're angry because I didn't come and say 'may I' or 'do I have your permission.' When you think logically about it, you'll be delighted. But you're so determined to be independent that . . ."

"I certainly am," she cut in. "And I won't let you dictate to me."

"Don't be childish."

Her breath caught in her throat. How could she make this man see what was wrong about his actions when he was fundamentally opposed to her freedom?"

"It has nothing to do with being childish," she said carefully. "Naturally I'm pleased to be free. What I'm not pleased about is that you went over my head to arrange it. Particularly when I asked you not to interfere."

"Is it interfering because I wish to make you my wife as soon as possible? You're behaving like this because you're angry at what happened yesterday. I have already apologized for that. I was jealous of your being with another man and . . ."

"I'll still lunch with other men friends even when I'm your wife," she said flatly.

"Only in our own home. No married woman dines out with another man unless her husband is with her."

The words fell with the sharpness of stones into a still pool, each one echoing in her mind and building up into a crescendo of sound.

"Let's go and sit by the pool," he said, and the carelessness with which he turned to leave showed he considered the conversation over.

It was all she needed to give her the courage she required. "You'd better go alone, Karim. I'm going upstairs to pack."

"To pack what?"

"My clothes. I'm leaving."

"Fleur." There was fond amusement in his voice. "Darling, I'm sorry I lost my temper again, but I hardly slept last night for worrying about you. It's made me short-tempered. Please forgive me." His hand stretched towards her. "Come."

"No! I'm leaving." He moved in her direction, but she drew back sharply. "Don't touch me, Karim. It's no use."

His brows drew together in anger. "I'm not a boy whom you can keep treating this way. I'm a man with a man's desire, and I'm holding it in check. Don't you know what a strain it puts on me when all I want is to take you?"

"Must you keep using those expressions! Is that the only way you can say you love me? Take . . . want . . . need . . . as if I'm an object that belongs to you!"

"You *do* belong to me!"

"Never. I belong to myself. I always have and I always will. I should never have got engaged to you. It was a mistake."

"Be quiet!" He lunged forward and gripped her shoulders. "You are overwrought and hysterical. You don't know what you're saying. We love each other, but we're tearing ourselves apart. Once you're my wife it will be different." His voice lowered, and the anger disappeared into tenderness, as if he were talking to a child.

And that's what she was to him, Fleur thought bitterly—a child and a sex object—not an intelligent woman with equal rights. How could she have imagined she would be happy with this man? To try and make him understand her was like trying to explain color to someone who had never seen.

"Go to your room and rest," he continued gently. "I will come up and see you in a little while."

"I don't want to rest. I want to leave."

"You don't mean it. You're only saying it because you saw your friend yesterday and he unsettled you. It's natural for him to want to put doubts in your mind."

She clutched at the thought of Rory, seeing him as her only means of escape. It would mean playing on Karim's jealousy, but it was the easiest way of getting him to release her without putting up a fight.

"It's because of Rory that I must go," she said hurriedly. "Seeing him again made me realize how much I've missed him. I . . . I hated the thought of his going back to England. It made me see I . . . that I care for him."

"I don't believe you. You love *me*—no one else." Karim's face was contorted with rage. "Say it. I want to hear you say it."

"I can't."

"You must. You love *me*. You can't marry anyone else."

"I can. I'm free to do as I want. And right now I want to be left alone."

"You're lying to me. I demand to know the truth. Do you love him or don't you? Is that what you're afraid to tell me?"

"Yes!" she cried, desperation driving her on. "I'm afraid. Afraid of the way you're trying to dominate me. Afraid of your temper and your jealousy. I mightn't reach the heights with Rory, but at least he won't make me feel degraded."

"Degraded!" Karim spat out the word as if it were poison. "You dare to say my love for you degrades you?"

"Yes!" She was too overwrought to care how much she hurt him. "You'd never let me exist as the person I am. You'd try and turn me into a copy of your mother— someone who'd have no life apart from her home and children. You only pretend to admire me because I'm independent. Once we were married you'd dominate me." Her voice cracked. "The way you're trying to do now. Look at you! Showing off how strong you are because you know your kisses won't get what you want."

"Enough!" he thundered. "I won't listen to any more."

"How typical!" she taunted. "Giving me orders and expecting me to obey them. That's the only way your mind works with women. Passion one minute and orders the next. You talk of women having the same rights as men, but you don't mean a word of it. If you did, you'd have tried to help Nizea instead of kowtowing to your father."

"Leave my father out of this." Karim stepped back from her as if he could not bear to touch her. "If your feelings for this Englishman are stronger than your feelings for me, then have the courage to say so without putting the blame on my family."

"I'm trying to make you see . . ."

"I've seen enough." He turned his back on her. "Go if you must. But no more talk. Not another word."

Swiftly she turned and ran to her room. She remained there until she heard Mr. and Mrs. Khan and Nizea drive away. Only then, with her case in her hand, did she go down to the hall in search of a servant.

She had no idea how she would reach Teheran but, if there was no public transport, she was desperate enough to hire a private car for the journey, regardless of the cost. She was halfway across the hall when Karim came out of the salon. He looked more like a statue than a person, so grave were his features.

"If you will tell one of the servants when you are ready to leave," he said quietly, "our helicopter will take you to Teheran."

"I'm ready to leave now."

For a brief instant a light flared in his eyes. "You've packed quickly."

"I left most of my clothes at Madame Nadar's."

"Will you be going back there?"

"Only until I can get a flight to London." She had answered his question without thinking but realized that what she had said was the truth. It would be impossible for her to remain anywhere near Karim, and the sooner she left this country, the sooner she would forget him.

"When is your friend going?"

She tried to remember what Rory had said. "In a couple of days' time, I'll . . . I'll call him as soon as I get to Teheran and see if I can get on the same flight."

With a nod, Karim went to the door and called to someone. A moment later the helicopter pilot appeared. He gave her a slight smile.

"I will take your luggage to the car," he said. "We can leave at once."

"Thank you." She waited until he disappeared with her case and then walked through the door, careful to keep as far away from Karim as possible.

"Good-bye," she whispered shakily, keeping her eyes

on the floor. "I . . . I'm sorry things had to end this way."

"It would have been more painful if we had already been married."

Knowing that had she been his wife she would never have had the courage to leave him, she went blindly down the steps and into the waiting car that would take her the half mile to the helicopter landing stage. She did not look back but resolutely stared ahead. From now she must never look back; never think of what might have been.

Was it possible for a person to live the rest of her life without a heart, she wondered, and knew that sometime in the years ahead she would find the answer, for she had left her heart with Karim Khan.

Thirteen

FLEUR *paid off the taxi and went* through the revolving doors leading to the offices of Benson & Bates. A pretty blond receptionist looked up at her approach.

"I have an appointment with Mr. Rory Baines," Fleur said.

"I'm not sure whether he's returned from holiday."

"He came back during the weekend. I saw him last night."

"You're better informed than I am," the girl smiled and motioned Fleur to sit down while she put a call through to him.

Ignoring the comfortable armchairs that decorated the foyer, Fleur went to stand by one of the windows. The traffic streamed past her along St. James's; cars and buses full of people going about their business, each one intent on his own affairs and not caring about anyone else. If only she could have such peace of mind. She knew she was being silly and that the people she was staring at probably had as many problems as herself. Yet she did not have any problems, she admonished herself. Once she could forget Karim, she would be fine.

As always his name brought back memories that stabbed her with pain. Karim kissing her and holding her, telling her how much he loved her; Karim begging her to forgive him for his jealousy and swearing that when she was his wife he would never doubt her. It was this kind of memory that darkened the other, happy ones and, if her months apart from him had taught her nothing else, it had shown her that her decision to leave him had been the right one. She loved him and would miss him all her life, but if she were faced with the same decision today, she would still leave him.

She moved slightly and the curtain at the window shifted, giving her a view of a heavily bearded man. He reminded her of Ibrahim Khan, and she wondered what he had said to Karim when he had learned of her departure. How pleased he must be with himself. And why shouldn't he, when he no longer had to face the prospect of an English daughter-in-law? He had been a wily opponent; not using his influence over his son but content to let events take their course, almost as if he had known she herself would be sufficient catalyst to destroy the situation.

"Mr. Baines will see you now," the receptionist called.

Fleur went to the elevator. She had not been here since Rory's marriage. How strange to think she could no longer regard him as her "old faithful." Little had she known when she had gone with him to the opera two months ago that she would meet an old school friend there with whom he would swiftly fall in love.

"Is he special?" Jenny had asked in a whisper when they met for drinks in the intermission.

"A specially good friend," Fleur had stated. "Nothing more. He's all yours if you can get him."

"I'll do my best," Jenny had said; and her best had been sufficient to make Rory propose within a month.

Now they had returned from their honeymoon in Bermuda, and Fleur was seeing Rory about the lease of a new flat she was taking. Once the contract was signed, her life would be settled on a new course. She sighed. A new course was exactly what she wanted, and the sooner everything was arranged, the better. Resolutely she pushed aside the self-pity that, over the last few weeks, kept welling up inside her. She knew it was only because it was October; the month she might have been Karim's wife.

I've got to stop thinking of him, she vowed. *He doesn't exist for me any more. I don't even like him. I never did.*

The elevator doors opened, and she stepped into the corridor.

"Hello, gorgeous!" It was Rory standing outside his office, tanned and beaming, and she was so delighted by the well-being that exuded from him that she ran toward him and flung her arms around his neck.

As she drew back she saw a man emerge from a room on her left. He was with someone else, but his dark gaze was fixed upon her and she was glad Rory's arms were still about her, otherwise she would have fallen.

"Karim!"

His nod was brief and included the man beside her.

"I heard you were due over this week," Rory smiled. "But I didn't realize you'd already arrived."

"I arrived last week," Karim replied. "I gather you've just returned from your honeymoon?"

"Yes. Two weeks in Bermuda—hence the tan." Rory glanced at Fleur and then pushed open the door of his office.

She stepped forward, then politeness forced her to speak to Karim. "How are your parents and Nizea?"

"My family are fine, thank you." His tone was formal, his glance still uncaring as he gave a casual nod and continued on his way.

Rory closed the office door, and Fleur collapsed into a chair. She knew Rory was watching her, but no amount of will-power could make her pretend she was unaffected by the sight of Karim. She felt shattered. He had looked at her as if she were a stranger. In the worst of her nightmares she had never seen his eyes so bleakly upon her.

"What was all that about?" Rory asked. "I thought you were going to faint when you saw him."

"I was surprised."

Rory sat at his desk. "I don't want to tread on corns, old girl, but would Karim Khan be the reason you rushed back from Iran? To begin with, I had hoped it was because of me, but I pretty soon knew it wasn't. Then I met Jenny and forgot everything except marrying her. But now I'm able to think rationally again . . ." He peered at her. "*Were* you in love with him?"

She nodded, not trusting herself to speak.

"Is he in love with you?"

"Does it look it?" she asked bitterly.

"No. But then you can never tell with people like Khan. He doesn't give his thoughts away."

She thought of the burning passion of Karim's mouth and knew how wrong this was. But she could not say so to Rory and instead thrust the contract at him. "Let's talk about this. That's what I'm here for."

"In other words, let's stick to business."

"Please, Rory, I don't want to talk about Karim. I was in love with him, and things didn't work out."

With a shrug Rory took up the contract and, for the next hour went through it carefully with her, pointing out the different clauses and suggesting she think them over before committing herself to them.

"It beats me why you want to buy a flat," he concluded. "I can't see your remaining single for long."

"Don't start matchmaking just because *you've* been hooked! I'm quite happy as I am."

"You're miles thinner," he commented. "I noticed it at the wedding, and it's even more noticeable now."

"You should have eyes only for your wife," she teased.

"It's because I'm so happy with Jenny that I look at other women with such affection!" His eyes rested on her breasts, their fullness more noticeable because of her slenderness. "I've never seen you in emerald green before," he added. "You look more like a model than a teacher."

"That's because I *am* a model."

"I don't believe you!"

"It's true. I felt teaching was getting me into a rut so I've given myself a year off to try my hand at other things. Modeling is one of them. I've already had a trip to Paris since you've been away, and this afternoon I'm going to see another agency that's interested in me."

"I bet they are," he said promptly. "But show me any contract before you sign it. I may be Jenny's old man, but I'm still your watchdog."

His teasing was good for her, and she could smile almost as if she meant it. She put the lease into her bag and stood up.

"Are you free for lunch?" he asked. "I have another appointment at two fifteen, but I've time for a snack."

"Suits me," she said, knowing she would sink into a depression if she were left alone.

Linking her arm through his in a deliberate gesture of gaiety, she walked with him to the elevator. Most of the partners and other clients were leaving the offices for the lunch hour and twice the elevator passed them, too full to stop. But on the third time the doors opened and they stepped in. Too late she saw Karim at the back, talking to a portly, silver-haired man whom she recognized as Sir Morgan Bates.

"Hullo, Rory," Sir Morgan said. "Glad to see you got back on time."

"I gathered that several bets had been taken that I wouldn't," Rory grinned. "I hope you didn't lose any money on me, sir?"

The elder man chuckled. "I knew Jenny wouldn't let you slack. Which reminds me, I'm dining with your father-in-law on Friday. Will you both be there?"

"Yes."

"Good. We'll talk then."

He resumed his conversation with Karim and, from the corner of her eye, Fleur saw Karim's face was pale, his eyes glittering so brightly that they seemed devoid of sight.

"As I was saying," Sir Morgan continued, "if we can get that merger . . ."

"Forgive me," Karim interrupted, "but would you mind if we canceled our lunch today?"

"Why . . . er . . . no. Is anything wrong, my boy?"

Before Karim could reply, the elevator reached the ground floor, and everyone moved out. Fleur pulled at Rory's arm, hoping he would increase his speed, but if anything he seemed to walk more slowly, and she was aware of Sir Morgan and Karim directly behind her.

"Fleur!" Karim's voice was like a bullet in her back, and she jerked but refused to stop.

"Fleur!" he called again. "I must talk to you. Are you free?"

"No." She clung to Rory's arm as if it were her salvation. "I'm lunching with . . ."

"Of course Fleur's free." Rory swiftly loosened her clinging fingers and placed them on Karim's arm.

She tried to draw back, but his hand came up instantly and gripped hers. "Excuse me, both of you," he said jerkily, looking from Rory to Sir Morgan. "I'll explain later. But first I've a few things to say to Fleur."

Swiftly he pulled her towards the entrance, moving with such speed that she had to run to keep up with him. Even when they reached the pavement, he did not stop but strode towards a black limousine parked by the curb.

"Get in," Karim ordered and pushed her none too gently into the back seat. He followed swiftly, as if afraid she would try to escape, and slammed the door. "Home," he said tersely, and the car immediately moved forward.

"Where are you taking me?" she demanded.

"Somewhere we can be alone. And don't argue, because I won't listen."

She remained silent throughout the journey, not because she was afraid of this man who was suddenly a stranger, but because she was afraid of what his nearness was doing to her. Obliquely she looked at him. In profile he looked even more forbidding than when she had seen him in the elevator. Deeply etched lines were carved down the sides of his nose, and there were shadows beneath his eyes. His skin too, had lost some of its glow and, now that a flush of anger was no longer staining it, seemed to be sallow, as if he had been ill and had not yet recovered. Her heart lurched and quickly she gazed ahead. It was not a moment too soon, for she felt him turn and regard her.

"You are more beautiful than ever," he stated flatly. "I have often thought about your hair and . . ." He stopped speaking and was silent for so long that she was surprised when he continued. "I remembered it as being the color of burnished gold, but I see memory has played me false. It has more red in it. It's like a flame."

"It only looks more red because I'm wearing a bright color." Her voice was thin, and she cleared her throat.

"In Persia you only wore pastel shades."

"I have a new image now." Her voice was still high. "I've given up teaching. I'm a model. Does that shock you?"

He did not answer, and she saw that the car was drawing to a halt outside a luxurious block of flats overlooking Hyde Park. The chauffeur opened the door, and Karim stepped out. He saw the quick glance she gave to her right as she followed him, and his fingers gripped themselves hurtfully around her arm.

"You're not escaping so easily," he muttered and pulled her forward.

"Please let go of me," she protested. "I promise not to run away."

Immediately he released his hold, and she walked beside him into the foyer and across to the elevator which took them swiftly to the top floor and an elegant apartment furnished in quiet good taste. But it was not Karim's taste, for there was nothing Persian about it.

"How long are you staying here?" she asked, deciding to open the conversation.

"In this apartment or in England?"

"Is there a difference?"

"I hope so." He hesitated and then flung his briefcase upon a chair. "I have this place on a monthly lease but I'm staying in England for some years."

"Years?" She could not believe she had heard him correctly.

"Five . . . ten . . . I don't know how long."

"But I . . . I . . . but your firm's in Teheran!" She was not aware of what she was saying. She only knew she had to say something.

"I have always wanted my firm to become an international one," he replied. "I told you so when we once discussed my work. I've been having talks with Sir Morgan for months. He's looking for a new senior partner and offered me the chance of it." He saw her astonishment. "You find it strange that he should want a foreigner?"

"Of course not. But I can't believe that you're willing

to leave Iran." Her eyes narrowed. "It does mean that, doesn't it?"

"Yes. I'll be keeping my Persian offices going, but in the main I'll be based over here."

"I can't believe it," she said again, and knowing it would be undiplomatic to say why, she stopped speaking.

"Why do you find it strange?" he questioned. "Because you can't see me fitting into the British way of life or because you're surprised I've left my father?"

"Mainly because of your father," she confessed and knew how bitterly Ibrahim Khan must resent his son's departure.

"My father was deeply disappointed," Karim said slowly, "but he is too keen for me to be successful to allow his disappointment to stand in my way. You find it hard to believe, Fleur, but I assure you he has only wanted my happiness."

"I'm sure of that," she said promptly, remembering how cleverly the old man had fought for it. "Is Ferada with you?"

There was a glint in his eyes. "You think I'd rush from your arms into those of another woman?"

"I can't see you remaining single forever."

"I'm glad of that. It gives me some hope for the future."

He moved closer. He was near enough to touch her, but his hands remained by his side. Unable to bear his proximity, she backed away and then walked towards the balcony. The park was milling with cars and people, and she could hear the muted sound of traffic.

"It must be quite noisy here during the rush hour," she said brightly. "But I suppose if you have double glazing it doesn't matter. Except in the summer, of course. But then you could have air conditioning."

"A third alternative," Karim said drily, "is to buy a house somewhere quieter. Knowing how much you like deciding things for yourself, I thought I would leave the decision to you."

She found it impossible to reply and went on staring through the window.

"Have you nothing to say?" he asked.

"I . . . I left you," she said slowly. "You let me go."

"Because I thought you were going to marry Rory. When I saw the way you flung yourself into his arms and kissed him this morning, I believed you were already his wife."

"Yet you expect me to believe you came to England because of me?"

"I knew you'd pick that one up." His voice was still dry. "I accepted Sir Morgan's offer the day after you agreed to become my wife."

Slowly she turned to look at him. "But all the talk about where we were going to live—the house we would buy in Teheran—even building a country villa—was all that a lie?"

"I intend to have a house in Teheran. I will need to go there on business and would hope to spend holidays there, too." He drew a deep breath as if to marshal his thoughts and set them before her in some order. "Even before I asked you to marry me, I had some idea of what your reaction would be. I know you enjoyed thinking I never understood you, but I assure you I understood you only too well." His voice deepened. "Sometimes painfully well. I knew you were afraid of my foreignness—please don't deny it—and all the things that made me seem so alien to you. You never stopped to consider that you were equally alien to me. But I loved you so deeply I didn't think our differences were important. I believed that together we'd forge a bond that would be a mixture of both our ways of life. The best of the East and the best of the West would be seen in our home and in our children."

"Oh, Karim." One of her hands lifted in his direction. "If only you'd said all this to me before."

"I only realized *that* when it was too late. I knew you were influenced by what my parents said and that you were afraid that once I'd possessed you, my love for you would weaken."

"You knew that?"

"Certainly. I also knew you were afraid of my father's influence over me. That also affected my decision. As long as I lived in Teheran, I would have to see him frequently. But if I lived abroad I need only see him when it suited me—and it still wouldn't offend him."

"But you love him," she cried. "You want to see him often."

"Not if it means I can't see *you*."

She drew a deep breath. "Is that why you accepted Sir Morgan's offer?"

"That's the main reason."

"Why didn't you tell me about it before?"

"I was planning it as a surprise. I wanted everything to be settled. Once it was, Sir Morgan was flying out to join us on the Caspian Sea for a holiday. You remember my father saying he was giving a party for the family?"

"Yes, but . . ."

"That's when I was going to tell you. Only the party never materialized because you left me."

He stopped speaking, and Fleur forced herself to look at him properly. Why was he standing so far away from her when the Karim of old would have been beside her, pulling her close, kissing her fiercely?

"You were lying when you said you were in love with Rory, weren't you?" he went on. "You used it as an excuse to leave me."

It was pointless to deny it now. "I was afraid that if I told you the real reason, you'd try to prevent me from going."

"And the real reason was my jealousy and possessiveness? That was what frightened you." He paused. "It still does, doesn't it?"

She went on looking at him. Karim in London seemed less frightening than Karim in his own country; but she was too muddled to know why.

"I can't answer you," she said tremulously. "My thoughts don't make sense."

"Perhaps I can help you." He moved forward but still stopped some distance away from her. "If we lived in my country, you would be surrounded by my culture and my people and would be afraid of losing your identity. You started to fear this during our engagement, and that made you turn me into an ogre. My stupid jealousy didn't help either," he added grimly, "and I've no excuse to offer for that."

He ran his tongue over his lips, and she noticed the movement with surprise, for it was the first indication he had given of nervousness. Karim afraid of *her?* It was an inconceivable thought. She looked at him steadily, beginning to understand what those lines upon his face meant; what had placed the shadows under his eyes; sprinkled the first gray on his temples. *Oh, my darling,* she thought tremulously. *And I believed I was the only one to suffer.* But Karim was continuing to speak, and she forced herself to listen.

"If we live in England," he said, "and I am surrounded by all your cool, stiff-upper-lip compatriots, maybe some of their attitude will rub off on me! I might not achieve quite the same phlegm, but I wouldn't be quite so possessive, either." His mouth thinned. "I remember you used the word 'obsessive' and I think you were right. But it's my obsession for you that has enabled me to put your happiness before everything else that I hold dear."

She swallowed hard. He had certainly done this. He had put her before his country, his family, even his work. Obsession it might be, but it was also an overwhelming love. But there was something else that didn't make sense, and she had to know the answer.

"Why did you continue with the move to England after I left you? Surely there was no point coming to London then."

"I couldn't bear to stay in Teheran," he said with quiet violence. "My father would have kept nagging me to marry, and it would have led to endless arguments. At least here I could live my lonely life and devote myself to work. Which I was prepared to do until an hour ago in the elevator when I suddenly discovered the wonderful truth." His eyes glittered. "No, I'm lying. I came to England hoping to make you change your mind and marry me. The day I arrived in London and went to Sir Morgan's office, I learned that Rory was on his honeymoon.

W'Allah!" There was a world of suffering in the word. "You'll never know the bitterness I felt. My life was shattered. In my mind I kept seeing you with him . . . saw him holding you, loving you."

His voice shook and, hearing the broken sound, Fleur flew across the room and into his arms. They came up immediately to hold her. He was trembling, unexpectedly vulnerable.

"How thin you are," he whispered, moving his hands gently down her shoulders to her waist. "A breath of wind could blow you away."

"Is that why you're afraid to kiss me?"

"I'm afraid that once I start, I won't be able to stop. And there are many things I want to say to you first."

"I don't need to hear any more. When I think of your coming here . . . of all you've given up . . ."

"Of all I've gained," he said huskily. "Think of that, my heart. It's much more important."

"I should never have left you." She clung to him and pressed her face upon his, not caring that he felt her tears. "I was stupid and ignorant. I thought *I* was the only one who knew how to love. I was afraid you only wanted me for . . ." She pressed closer to him, unwilling to continue.

"For your body?" he said. "And did you also think that once I possessed it, I would grow tired of it?" He put his hands on either side of her temples. "I think that's what my father wanted you to believe. I won't answer such an accusation. Time will do it for me."

"Your willingness to live here has already done it," she murmured.

"Good. Then I won't be accused of lust if I insist on an

immediate marriage! You once agreed to be my bride in October, and we only have twelve days left in which to make the arrangements."

"Can it be a quiet wedding?" she pleaded. "I know you'll want it to be back home, but . . ."

"No," he interrupted. "It will be here. My parents and Nizea will fly over for it. I've no intention of taking you to Teheran until we've been married long enough for you to have confidence in your power over me."

"In our power over each other," she corrected, and felt the deep shudder that went through him as he pressed his mouth against the softness of her neck.

"When we're married," he whispered, "would you mind if Nizea came to live with us?"

"You mean she's coming to England?"

"She has been accepted for the university. I persuaded my father to let her live here with me."

"I can't believe any of this is happening." Fleur put her arms under Karim's jacket. "When I woke up this morning all the world was dark and miserable, and now it's exploding into a thousand glorious lights."

"There's only one light in *my* world," he said, "and that's you, my flower of the desert."

"I can't be a flower of the desert if we live in London."

"Then let's say you're the flower of my heart."

She laughed, but the sound was stifled as his lips covered hers. The long months of their separation were not going to be easily assuaged and neither of them attempted it, knowing that this would not be until they were man and wife. But they were content to remain close, to murmur endearments, to kiss gently, and to savor their newly discovered understanding of each other. There might be difficulties ahead, but nothing would be too great for their love to surmount.

"Apart we are nothing," Karim whispered, echoing her thoughts. "But together we are everything."

FREE
Fawcett Books Listing

There is Romance, Mystery, Suspense, and Adventure waiting for you inside the Fawcett Books Order Form. And it's yours to browse through and use to get all the books you've been wanting . . . but possibly couldn't find in your bookstore.

This easy-to-use order form is divided into categories and contains over 1500 titles by your favorite authors.

So don't delay—take advantage of this special opportunity to increase your reading pleasure.

Just send us your name and address and 35¢ (to help defray postage and handling costs).